THE
CLARINET WHALE

KIMBERLY SAILOR

This is a work of fiction. All of the characters, organizations, and events portrayed in this novel are either products of the author's imagination or are used fictitiously.

THE CLARINET WHALE

For permissions, media requests, sales information, or related questions, use the "Inquires" tab at: www.theclarinetwhale.com.

Cover design and editorial coordination by
Little Creek Press, a division of Kristin Mitchell Design, LLC

Copyediting by Carl Stratman

LCCN 2014920421
ISBN 978-0-692-33085-2

First Edition: December 2014
First Printing: January 2015

10 9 8 7 6 5 4 3 2 1

THE
CLARINET
WHALE

KIMBERLY SAILOR

CHAPTER
1

I am still alive.

I break into St. Paul's around seven. Why do churches lock so early? It's just past dinnertime. If they'd stay open later I wouldn't have to resort to security codes and trespassing. Surely some devotees would like to come down to pray after dessert. My fingers follow their learned pattern on the touchpad—seven, three, seven, one—and the door clicks open, just for me.

It's cold in here. Why are churches so cold? I suppose they have to save on the heat bill, especially when there's fleeting members. I pull my hood over my head, casting a playful monk image on suburbia. My reflection joins me in the foyer, creeping along the nursery room window, gliding over the choir room's double doors. I'm grateful for the thick inviting carpeting since it softens my noisy sandals. It definitely makes me feel less criminal to go about this quietly, nearly reverently.

I enter the sanctuary to greet the guardsmen, the Apostles. This church has crude plastic replicas of The Twelve nailed to its walls. My mind wanders back to the days of Sunday School and my Bible lessons. But I can't remember much theology from Sunday School. I mostly remember little slices, the leftover memories. I remember hot roast beef sandwiches for our annual picnic. I recall decorating a wreath as a class for Christmas—I made little paper doves that nestled in the real pine needles. There were workbooks with fill-in-the-blank questions about Jesus. Every year I gave up candy for Lent.

I still have the images of prayer memorization charts and affixing red stars in my mind, and some hazy recollection of being a teenager in Sunday School. The teen years included a lock-in night and confirmation workshops with the nun. Boy, did we give that nun hell. A stout woman with thin lips, she only lasted two years before her relocation pleadings were mercifully answered by the Bishop. But of all the eras in my life, I recall the least about being a teenager. I can tell you what I received for each birthday from age six to twelve, but past that, nothing much. Just a few vacation memories, since we were always traveling. Outside from one particular incident at eighteen, nothing really bubbles to the top of my mind until my twentieth birthday, and perhaps that one only stands out because it was a new decade of my life, and because I recently acquired my first (and last) boyfriend.

Josh was my best friend in preschool. Amy was my best friend in first grade. I realized I needed glasses in fourth grade. I made folder forts on my desk in fifth grade. I remember it all, everyday details about school and life, and then next to nothing. Could I remember if I let myself?

I walk up to the apostle Peter, but only because he's the closest. I don't play favorites with these guys, even though Peter was the first pope, Jesus's pope. Peter's artist gave extra attention to his garb, the white plastic nicely sculpted to make Peter's robe look flowing and textured. There are even little patterns on the robe, which would probably be lace trim in real life. Peter with lace trim? Should we give him a fancy handkerchief, too? My hand touches his robe, as it has a hundred times before. I think I'd like to see Peter in blue. I think Peter deserves a pair of proper shoes after all these years. I'd like to place my hand on his cheek, but his cheek is just too small. I place a finger there instead, slowly moving down like the path of a tear. Peter's face is molded into a permanent frown. I want to place my fingers over his lips and push them up, but I don't dare. His eyes haunt. His ears sag gently. Was Peter part of my teenage years? I think he'd have salt and pepper hair. I think he'd have a radio voice. I do know I used to pray to Peter, but I don't do much praying these days.

I creep along between the pews. There are many to visit in this church. After my hellos are passed to the remaining Apostles, there are books to embrace. I pick up dusty hymnals, picking at golden edges as I kiss leather covers. I scoop up prayer books, swiftly reading my favorite psalms in numerical order. I scan the new bulletin, seeing what next week has in store for the church. But the Bibles, those I leave alone. The Bible has terrified me since that summer after high school. If I learn too much, I risk the possibility of putting a name to this sin, or discovering a character in Biblical history who shares my present, who has my traits. I'm not ready for this connection. I recognize that this makes me weak and ignorant, but self-preservation must be taken into account. So the Bibles remain neatly tucked away in their wooden holders. Between now and the next time I'm here I'll put the Bible out of my mind, as I always do. And if I happen to be here on Sunday, I'll decide that the Bible is really just an encyclopedia or yearbook. That is, if I end up in church on Sunday. So far I've been here every night this week after the dinner plates are put away, but there's always an excuse come Sunday. I have to make chicken stock. I forgot my files on campus. The cat is acting oddly, I should stay home.

I take my usual spot in the first row to rest. This church is really quite remarkable. I know that the architecture is meant to please

God, show him he's worth it. I know that members give more when they're giving to something really beautiful and sturdy. I feel a bit of cynicism toward this, but all the same, I too am inspired when I see thick, carved pillars and a soaring cathedral ceiling. I get excited knowing that when viewed from above, this church is in the shape of a cross. Now that's holy engineering. I feel humbled when I see stained glassed windows larger than a bus, carefully designed and created by real craftsmen with real skill. I have to stop and think about my life when I see hundreds of shiny cherry wood pews, so tidy and inviting, yet filled for just one hour per week. And a marble altar so perfect, so commanding, is nearly perfect enough to instigate calls to old friends who faded away, to tell them all I'm sorry and let's just start this whole thing over again. And a cross so sturdy, so high, with a person so familiar hanging from it, is almost enough to make me change all that's wrong. Almost.

I joined St. Paul's when I moved to Ann Arbor. I really wanted to try a few churches before I committed, as denominations mean very little to me, though the congregation does. I have certain evaluative criteria to apply to potential church homes. Mostly, the congregation can neither be too progressive nor too regressive, and the choir has to sing in tune. Am I really "breaking in" to a church if I'm on its member roster?

I float to the altar. The church is so quiet on Friday nights. I wonder what God is up to on Friday nights when people get rowdy downtown. It's so still in here, so very still, that it makes me nervous. I keep expecting the chandelier to fall from the ceiling, smashing crystals across the pews and marble. Wouldn't that be a dramatic sight to watch from above? And every once in a while, I expect the organ to start playing by itself. Some booming, dissonant concerto. One of those loud, uncomfortable pieces that makes you think Satan is on his way. Or, sometimes I think that a water pipe will burst, and then another, and then every pipe in the city, and Noah's Ark will come cruising in as the rescue squad. This is wild, I know. But that's how quiet it is in here on Friday nights; it's so quiet that I've come to expect a disaster just to disturb this profound peace that can't possibly be real.

I walk the sacred steps at the front of the church. I'm a trespasser, I tell myself again. I tell myself this every time I act up, but it hasn't made a difference yet. And there's no red carpet to soften my steps up here, so I've got to be really quiet just in case someone is around. Really, I'm no better than a Peeping Tom or a high school kid toilet papering another house by moonlight. Actually, I'm much worse than they are.

My eyes are on the gold cabinet now. I round the altar, vision fixated. With soft hands I turn the key, the cup and bowl waiting for me. I take out the Communion wafers, take out Jesus's body; his armless, legless body. I carry the Communion bowl back to the altar. Holy work must be conducted on holy ground. I remove three pieces, my personal trinity, and place them into my purse. My eyes shoot up in a moment of fear, quickly scanning the sanctuary. No one's here but the Apostles.

It'd sure be empowering to kick them out and have the whole church to myself.

The Apostles awaken at this, but they've got other projects to work on, closer deadlines to meet, and seem only lightly embarrassed over that last thought.

I can see my potential audience now, the members of this church, if I were the priest. In the front, with suits on the men and two-piece silks on the women, are the wealthy sinners. I think they're my favorite. I find pretentiousness rather enviable. I love fanciness. And I'm a bit snobbish myself. This group makes me delighted—inspired even, respectful of their money and poise. I'd be sure to smile at them lovingly if I was delivering the Word, counting on continued donations.

Families with children sit in the middle, which is probably the worst place for squirming vocal kids, but this is where they usually end up because the popular seats in the back are gone by the time they all rush in. The parents talk with their play group and potluck friends before the procession starts. These folks sing too loudly, and they're a noisy mess with jackets and diaper bags and toys before you even consider their children. A few mothers have to leave during the service, their screaming infants no longer charming. Their toddler children remain and stare at others, noses dripping, mouths chewing on father's shoulder. "Hey, don't bite!" Dad reminds them. Many are starter families, attractive families, some with cheating husbands. The church needs these cheating husbands, because everyone likes to be saved and they'll pay good money for the chance.

Finally, a hodgepodge group makes up the back. They are the widowed, the single, the ones with complicated stories. They are the men who insist on sitting in the back to make a quick exit, and they are the socially scared who would rather not be seen. Plus, the criminals sit in back. When I go to church, I sit in back. I try to stay out of sight of our priest, Father Duling. If he ever looked me right in the eyes, I bet something would happen. Maybe something really great, like I'd see the eyes of Jesus and stop this foolishness. But more likely, I'd see the eyes of Satan and really lose my mind. I sometimes hear whispers of "reformed" people in our church, but I know there are active criminals mingling, too.

My audience stands before me as I walk down the center aisle, away from the altar. It's like being an actor in a play. Or a teacher. A lot of churchgoers here aren't that educated, despite the university setting, which makes their church a classroom experience. The priest thus serves as a lecturer, a professor, and many of his pupils do take notes on the bulletin with little yellow pew pencils. This terrifies me, because everyone knows there are some bad professors out there. Some professors are even lunatics who teach history wrong on purpose.

The Apostles yawn at my dated assessment.

It's just me and the empty church again. I check my watch, now showing seven-thirty; I won't be expected home from my walk until eight. I reach into my pocket and pull out the church's indoor skeleton key as I head to the back. With a sharp crack the reconciliation room pops open. Extra nervous now, I scan the church for new bodies. I'm still mostly alone. I slip in, the door clicking to safety a moment later.

Though I'm in confessional booths weekly, I've never confessed anything here. Maybe because I've never had a priest with me, but mostly because I'm too ashamed. I merely sit and think about matters, sometimes vaguely pleading for assistance without being too specific. I suppose I could quietly confess aloud, but Catholics say it's not good enough unless the priest hears you. For me, religion both fascinates and frustrates, but rarely frees. I remain tormented.

It's beautiful in this little room. It has ivory and gold wallpaper, and red candles that make me feel particularly safe and remorseful at the same time. Sometimes, at the right time of year, you can see the moon through the oval window. It's hauntingly beautiful, as if Heaven herself is watching her second home, like this is a pleasant vacation property down south. There's even a tiny altar in here, presumably for the really serious sinners. Sometimes I consider kneeling there, but that seems even more criminal for a woman in my situation. *Lord, replace these memories with better ones,* I plead in my head. There I go, with the pleading.

I sneak out and slip down the side stairs. Outside the air revives me, and reminds me that spring is underway. April is a beautiful month, especially in Ann Arbor.

*

Inside St. Paul's Church, Father Duling was just in time to see Mae Harrington's back disappear into the evening. His teeth clench. With aged steps he climbs the altar, pattering slowly to the corner. He gingerly removes the Communion bowl, lifting the lid and tipping it close. Empty, as suspected.

"Maybe the Catholic Church isn't the best fit for you," Father Duling once told her, even though the very words brought him immediate pain. "Some churches are less . . . formal," he said. "You might be more comfortable elsewhere."

It was probably easy enough for her to get the skeleton key from the back supply room, but obtaining those security codes is a more serious matter. He descends to the confessional room, knowing she certainly went in there, too. Thankfully she's never destroyed or defaced anything, with her mind so ill and her fit body so capable of causing worlds of damage. He prays for her, that she'll settle the demons in her head and process the events of her youth with clarity and a new sense of direction. But he's also deeply suspicious of Mae, of her living arrangement with that younger boy from campus and her seemingly endless addiction to tampering with the church, and finds himself passing judgment on the one who seems incapable of righting herself.

CHAPTER 2

I'm an English professor at a university of 45,000. Library jobs, several thousand pounds of hardcover literature read, and two advanced degrees allows me to stand in front of thirty freshmen five days a week.

I often receive poor evaluations from my students because my required reading is too "obscure" or "unnecessary," or my favorite, "irrelevant." I don't assign much that's modern or hip. I don't assign articles that change the "national conversation." But they'll return to ancient literature during times of crisis, because the difficult words and strange language style will make them focus on something other than themselves. And maybe they'll remember me, and think a little better of me. They'll listen to their spouses sleeping, wishing the in-and-out sound belonged to someone else. They'll pack for a family vacation, missing their hedges and flatware and ocean shower curtain before they've left the driveway, knowing that vacations bring the worst out of that same spouse. And so they'll read, something from long ago that takes their minds off of today.

I walk down State Street toward the university. The campus vibe follows you, watches you, walks along with you. It's a voyeur, with Ann Arbor's streets neatly weaving in and out of little tucked-away places where students slide into, those eyes still everywhere. I pass taco stands, boutique shoe stores, and guys in frayed jeans playing guitars. I walk among men in suits and women in heels alongside girls with backpacks and teens on skateboards. Campus is huge, and campus inspires. There's always an energized bustle, and a sense of in-progress mischief making. There are sorority girls taking hits behind the General Education Building, and scientists on laptops at lunch. Pedestrians are everywhere, all with distraction in their eyes. Political rallies crescendo and decrescendo in the morning, with protestors trying to save a group of orphans in foreign cities that no one at the rally has ever visited. By noon, leaflets drop from the bookstore about fair prices and labor disputes. Boys fall in love with their best friend's ex-girlfriend while stem cell research advances by evening. Math teachers sleep with chemistry teachers, and blown generators shut down cafeterias for dinner. Everything that is jarring and extraordinary to citizens off campus is expected and delightful to citizens on campus. Campuses are sinful, but are worshipped through sports and medicine and discovery. They are their own cities, with their own agendas. I love the school scene, and enjoy visiting new campuses when I travel; it's comforting to compare and walk among the familiar. I don't get homesick for or talk about Minnesota much, which is where I grew up, and that's probably because I just shifted from one college town to another my whole life.

And here on my campus, another day passes, as it has in some identifiable fashion for nearly two hundred years.

I slip into a city bus around six. Couples and families are on the streets, some ducking into restaurants, others laughing their way out with stacks of take-out boxes. The bus driver is an elderly black man. A fragile older woman sits near him. Both read the obituary section today, and both have something to say about it. "Can you believe he was only fifty-seven? So young. Just a baby," the bus driver says. Both shake their heads and mourn briefly. "Remember fifty-seven?" the old woman asks, perking up. "Fifty-seven was so fun! Boy was it great to be young and fifty-seven."

It's an easy walk home from my bus stop. I feel less guilty about stealing Communion bread from St. Paul's as the roads change from avenues to streets. As I turn the corner onto my own street, I tell myself that I'll never break into another church again. Especially one where I'm already a member. How completely unnecessary and loony.

My neighbor is having a rummage sale, his yard full of mismatched dishes and dated curtains, a few side tables, board games, tablecloths, and a large chest with tiny drawers that immediately catches my eye. I cross the road to inspect the piece, which is nearly a library card catalog, but less utilitarian and more beautiful with its shiny cherry wood and heavy silver knobs. There's probably thirty compartments, and a deep top shelf that could hold a lot of something I've been storing in my dresser.

"How much for this?" I ask Dale, running my fingers along the grain.

Dale smiles, "Well Mae, I just want to get rid of it. It's getting dark and I'm ready to close up here. Take it for ten? I'll even help carry it over."

Soon the piece is set gingerly on my porch, awaiting Jack's help to get it inside.

The house is still. Lights off, chairs empty, air eager for human breath. I enjoy this house. It's big, it has character, and it makes me feel like I've lived a good life even if I didn't earn this house. My property sits on the craggy banks of a Huron River inlet. I have a lovely, unobstructed view of the slim passage. In the summer, little rowboats drift by, men with fishing lines working the shallow waters. In the winter, I see nothing but stark gray and silver for long passes in either direction, without a building or person to watch or wonder about. It's a very peaceful, unique neighborhood for a large town. It makes me realize that, in a roundabout way, I'm five minutes from the middle of nowhere. And sometimes, I need to be five minutes from the middle of nowhere.

I sit in the pending darkness, content to watch waterway happenings on display out my bay windows. It's rather peculiar to be home alone at this hour. I should make use of this unexpected alone time. I could organize my notes for class or grade papers. I could go through my books and weed out ones I'll never look at again, or try to make sense of the mail piling up on the ledge. But normal matters can be done in the company of Jack.

Instead, I'll go count my bread. And now, thanks to Dale, I have a new chest of drawers to store every last crumb.

My cat Oscar turns the corner to see me, his tail up and flicking. "Hey old-timer," I whisper, reaching down to scratch his back. I walk through the dining room, turning the corner into the lower hallway. I continue to Jack's doorframe where I pause for a moment. His floor supports classical music albums, tight jeans, scribbles of poetry, and a condom wrapper. Oh to be twenty-two again. I quickly make his bed and turn down the sheets, leaving before I crack and snoop. The last time I snooped, I found all sorts of horrors and wonders, which left my mind cluttered and my heart confused for weeks. No more snooping in Jack's room. He is, after all, my tenant. I really shouldn't be making his bed either, I decide as I head up the stairs.

My room has less humanity. A giant oak bed for one, a giant oak dresser for one. Bare hardwood floors. Nothing whatsoever on the walls. Sparse, but comfortable, and very tidy. I approach the dresser, pulling open the third drawer as I have for the past two years. I'm amazed that I'm not more careful about this. I should really keep my bread locked up. The churches lock theirs; why don't I? But the only person who could discover my collection is Jack, and his preoccupation with himself should keep him out of my things and out of harm's way. I find the wooden box I'm searching for behind my skirts. I place the box on my bed, eager to take inventory and feel satisfaction about my increasing reserves. I pull out today's haul from my purse, sorting the wafers on my white quilted bedspread.

The air is wet now, the Huron creeping through my open windows. I pull on a sweatshirt when I finish and creak back down the stairs and into my office, which is adjacent to Jack's room. With a flip of a switch, my achievements and setbacks are illuminated: diplomas, handwritten letters, a photo taken in Chicago. I sit in my chair, sullen. I hate the gloaming. Days go by so quickly. Jack says I've never gotten over my first love and that's why I hate evenings, which should be bustling with family ongoings instead of being so quiet. This is completely unwarranted for him to say, and besides, I've always hated evenings. He's getting a little too bold lately. I like to think that his upcoming graduation has got him, God forbid, *feeling* something, but everyone knows that Jack feels nothing. His complete apathy and recklessness changed the way I see people. He is devastatingly attractive, soundly brilliant, and completely full of curiosity. But I've watched him throw girls around, girls who willingly get naked for him, girls whom he later poisons with his insincerity. He gets the girl to have a crush on him. Too soon, a dependency on him. They share deep thoughts in the backyard, walk onto my pier to do whatever, and buy breakfast together at dawn. He leaves his girls voicemails that say, "You've come into my life just when I needed you most," a week before he tells them, "I've met someone else." *Even if there is no one else.* I just take a little bread away, but Jack takes souls away.

I open my laptop, ready to at least record test grades. My fingers click-clack while my mind visits last week. My few friends tell me that they're impressed, startled, and shocked when they reflect upon the last year of their life. I'm impressed, startled, and shocked when I reflect upon the last day of my life. Nothing of great magnitude has happened to me in years, but the more secretive I've become, the more outsiders tell me everything that happens to them. It's like a forced balance in the universe; I'm quieter, so more noise must be made. And I love and hate that people choose to confide in me. "You never judge, just listen," they tell me. Oh, but I judge. I judge myself against them, comparing their stories to the ones in my head and to what's happened to me. Their confessions mold me, haunt me, challenge me. But I don't react in front of them. That's my signature: stay flat. I guess that's why people keep trusting me with their own revelations and secrets.

I stand to brew a pot of tea. I can tell I'm too strained with mental ongoings to sleep tonight. I hear the front door open. Jack, young and loud, clatters through the living room and past his room. "Mae," he says, eyes shining with force. "Mae, are you alright?"

My stomach flips. "What are you talking about?"

"Didn't you hear? The Pope is about to die."

*

Night explodes in my bedroom. Crickets, and the ticking clock, and the creaking bed springs. I can never sleep on the weekends. Why? Over-fatigue from the week's close? Anxiety over the coming week? I'm scratching the fur on Oscar's head when my door clicks open.

Jack seems to float across the floor, pausing at my dresser.

"Are you awake?" he whispers.

"Yes."

He lies on top of the covers, warmer and stronger than me.

"I thought maybe we could talk for a while," he says. I nod, and though it's dark, he sees me.

"So the universe is rapidly expanding . . ." he starts.

"Oh Jack. No super deep thoughts tonight. Nothing galaxy-level."

He tries again. He always tries again, even when I resist. He just wants to talk, wants some company, but can't do it gracefully. We've fallen into this tradition of talking about big concept stuff, because it isn't too personal, isn't too painful. "What about life expectancy? Which generation will be the first with a life expectancy of one hundred?"

I hesitate, listening to the night again. "You know I hate talking about death."

"I didn't say anything about death. I said 'life' expectancy. I didn't say 'death,' you did," he accuses. "It comes to your mind first because you're scared to die. I thought Christians weren't really afraid of that because of their promised afterlife."

He waits. "Maybe you're not Christian."

His words hurt. I think of my bread. I think of my mother, and father, and people in history books who seem so amazing and permanent, but are gone now. Just gone. Where have they gone? How can leaders and thinkers and parents just come and go? I keep thinking. I think about repenting. I wonder if there's another way to save myself.

"You know," I start, though take moments before I begin again. "You know, I never used to be scared of dying."

"I know," he whispers. "I think I saw a glimpse of the other you when we first met. You were less aloof then."

The other me. I think he's referring to the one who taught him British literature when he was a freshman. He sat in the back, reading Arthur Miller instead because he'd read so far ahead in my required reading list that he was out of assigned books. "Jack, pay attention!" I'd scold. "And put the American away! Couldn't you pick something on topic, or at least from the right era?" He'd sigh and sit up, listening to me getting worked up about pastoral settings and royalty. I liked Jack. I liked his feistiness, his intelligence. I liked that he had an addiction to learning and was good at keeping himself busy. He was looking for a place to stay after that semester, and I was looking to rent out a room. I needed to fill the house, to add someone.

But, I was definitely already scared of dying by the time we met. I was just more healthy then, and all of this was less apparent.

"I think about death all the time," I say. "Some days it's really positive. Death can scare me enough to move me. To leave the house early, to be energetic, and to talk to people and think about people and miss people because some day, they're going to be missing me. But some days I'm so scared of death that I don't do anything except sit and worry. I won't do anything special or interesting or even necessary because I know I'm just going to die anyway. Also, language permits precision, and I don't think I'm 'aloof.'"

Jack waits. He stirs. He breathes. He says, "Is this why you won't love again? Because mortality gets in the way? Because nothing is forever?"

Jack has compelling ideas. Jack is quite perceptive for choosing to play the field. I'm not sure what to say, so I say nothing. Instead, I think of the living.

"You know," I realize, trying to tip it back to generalness, "I think our life expectancy should already be one hundred."

"Oh?" he says.

"But we're inbred, so most of us can't reach one hundred.

Especially those of us closely inbred."

I hear his silent processing. "What?"

"How else do you explain race-specific disease?" I say.

Jack exhales. I can still hear him thinking, the silent mechanic.

"Don't get going too fast," I tell him. "Just trying to get you worked up. Just trying to get myself a little worked up again about something other than me."

"Hey, are you going to watch the Pope's funeral?" he says, leaning in.

We don't have a television. "Seems doubtful. Where would I go to watch? A sports bar? An electronics store?"

"Well for heaven's sake, you have colleagues. Watch it at someone else's house."

Jack knows things. He knows my guilt about religion. He's clearly aware of my obsession over religion if he thinks the Pope's death might do me in. But I've never let him know exactly what he'd like to know.

"Jack . . . do you think you're a reincarnated spirit?"

"Very unlikely."

"Why?"

"Because I don't believe in reincarnation. I don't believe in anything, if you recall."

"You believe in me," I say.

He smiles. "But if you were a religion, I wouldn't."

CHAPTER
3

I wake very early. I turn on my stomach. I get to thinking. Twelve springs have come and gone since Brian left me. We met in college. He came in a high school valedictorian, and left a college valedictorian. He was "that hot guy from down the hall," a tall boy from Kansas with just a touch of madness. I found him particularly compelling because he had strong Midwestern values, but looked like a classic California surfer, complete with a glistening year-round tan and fluffy blonde beach hair. He sang baritone, even though he should have sang tenor. He bought me groceries and fed my cat when I was in class. We toured the missions in Santa Barbara, saw symphonies on Fridays, and biked to the movies with me on his handlebars. We drank port and smoked cigars on the roof of the Journalism School. I wore his sweatshirts and he gave me quarters for laundry. He made friends with my friends, and promised me a ring. He told me I'd make a beautiful mother, and that our boys would be Boy Scouts.

His voice. It haunts. I can still hear him belting high notes, somehow, like his voice is carrying all the way to me among the sirens and rattling garbage trucks of the city. He never thought he was particularly exceptional, but I heard all the makings of an opera star in his car and in the rain of his shower. His words. They kill. "I want to take care of you," he'd say. "I want to see Ireland with you, and sing across Austria with you," he'd continue as we drove down the 405 at night. California was so exhilarating for us Midwestern kids. "I'm going to save you," he promised. "I'm going to save you from everything safe and give you an extraordinary life."

Then he called me on an unfolding Sunday. It was just after sunrise, and I was lost under my comforter, happy to be warm and think about brunch plans between dreams. We were living in separate states then, doing separate graduate work and trying to separately grow our day-to-day ventures into something bigger. "I can't be with you anymore," he said, his voice groggy with alcohol. "I've met someone else."

"When?"

"Last night," he said.

I've never dated anyone since, and I never will. I told him that he's the only one I'd ever love. I did not lie. He made me mad. He made me love a lot less. He made me asexual, and an A-student. But mostly, he just made me, and this is the way I am now.

I walk to the shower. I notice myself as I undress. I've always loved my skin—it's a perfect shade, and still so flawless. I keep waiting for veins and bumps and dryness, but it never happens. My legs are shapely, my arms thin, my stomach tight with faint muscles showing. My bright blue eyes are unnaturally large, and my thick brown hair always waves evocatively. My mind might be compromised, but I'm a thirty-six-year-old knockout. And a good body counts for a lot when your mind is a mess. My reflection gets me through many gloamings, and many sins, because I'm happy I have something I'm pleased with. I once told Brian, "I bet you're never lonely with a voice like yours. You can just sing melodies when you want company." My personal happiness is wondering why I'm aging so slowly, so easily, despite the second life I lead in my head.

My shower is hot, and strange. I think it's too early to be up. I think I should go out for lunch. I think I'd like some wine with breakfast. The porcelain tiles seem to shift beneath my feet as I towel dry, unstable from my anxiety.

I robe and leave. Jack is sitting on his floor, shirtless and awake. I stand in the doorframe, curious. I watch as he slowly raises his arm, his limp hand turning into a fist. Then the first arm lowers as the other rises. This time, he lifts his knees to his chest when he makes a fist.

"Are you actively meditating again?" I ask.

"Shh," the twenty-two-year-old says.

I watch the floor acrobatics continue. I listen as his inhalations grow louder and louder, as though he were about to yell, but he never does. Jack flips to his stomach, arching on his imaginary wave.

"Do you want eggs or pancakes for breakfast?" I try again.

"Shh," he tells me before rolling on his side.

"Why don't you try yoga? Why don't you take a class on campus? You look silly," I tell him as he rolls onto my feet.

"Listen," he says from the floor. "I moved that big-ass chest of drawers from Dale into your house all by myself. I need to cool down. That was a workout. I hope it's fine in the dining room, because it'll never get up the stairs unless it sprouts wings." He rolls away into the splits, raising his hands like a sprinter who just crossed the finish line. "And I'll have an epiphany for breakfast," he says from the corner, happy to get an eye roll from me.

"Also, you know you invited Sam and Julie over for breakfast, right?" he continues. "Let's worry about that, since you told them to be here at seven. Who says seven on a Saturday? The things I do for you."

I scurry to the kitchen. My anxiety ends. Jack set the table. Jack has eggs and sausage and bacon warming under the stove's light. Jack even brought in cut tulips from the yard.

It's hard not to care for him.

Sam and Julie knock soon, a newspaper in Julie's hand, a small television in Sam's.

"I know you don't like the Devil Box," Sam says, "But today is very important. As thinkers and activists, as fucking professors, we're supposed to be informed," he says dramatically. "It is our civic responsibility, and our global goddamned duty," he concludes before plugging in the television.

"I just love your home," Julie says. "I feel peaceful when I'm here. I love the colors—the deep reds and soft yellows. I love the antiques and the metal—it's old meets new. I love the touches of country and city. And I especially like the wood moldings. I've been reading a lot of decorating journals lately," she admits.

So this is what other women think about.

I met Sam and Julie in a rather typical academic manner. I was working as a library assistant in a campus library, and they were Saturday morning regulars. I approached them one day, curious about their interests. "Today we're learning about Dostoevsky's life," they said.

"He used to be one of my favorites," I admitted. I bought them lunch that day. The next week, they bought me dinner. We've been getting together about every week since. That was six years ago. Sam teaches physics and Julie teaches fine arts.

The morning passes. Images blink on and dash off, voices of correspondents come and go. We watch our assembled package— a timeline of the Pope's reign in photographs and clips and stories—snapping off bacon and chiming in with church anecdotes. "I went to this church picnic in high school as a service project,"

Sam begins, "I was volunteering—setting up games, serving food, you know. And the priest was from another country. Can't remember where exactly, but somewhere in South America. He was the only colored person in the whole town. But that's another story. Anyway, he started drinking this delicious cold beverage called 'beer'—his very first time drinking beer! He downed a couple of bottles of local stuff, good and strong, and that's when the church picnic really got started. Some crazy parishioners taught him a few song and dance numbers behind the big tent. An hour later, he was doing a solo polka, a huge grin on his face, and the song, 'In heaven there is no beer, that's why we drink it here!' was firing out of his mouth."

On the television, a clip of the Pope addressing a crowd plays.

"Well get this," Julie says. We turn our attention to her, watching the petite blonde get ready. "When I was six, I was the lead angel in the Christmas play. The play director told us to come to the church in our outfits to save time. I must have been incredibly nervous, because the lead angel had to sing *Silent Night* all by herself. I slipped on my white robe and pulled on my sparkling angel wings, completely forgetting to put clothes on underneath. So after the play, when all the children were returning their costumes, I stood in the corner alone, aware of my mistake and hoping to slip out the back door to the parking lot. But the director caught me and I had to tell her what happened. She told me to stay in my outfit, wings and all, and go find my parents in the pews. It was so humiliating walking through the church. Everyone was whispering and chuckling at the lost angel. As I was crawling over people in my pew, it got so much worse when the tip of my wing cut the back of someone's neck. It was an old woman, who cried out and looked pissed. Everyone's eyes were on me, the naughty little angel. So you know what I did?"

"What did you do?" Sam asks, completely fascinated by the story he's hearing for the first time.

"I made an announcement," Julie tells us. "I said, 'Sometimes angels forget their manners and forget their clothes.'"

My friends howl, while I wonder how Julie can remember all of that from early childhood. On television, a tour of the crypt begins.

"I've got one," Jack says, his strong arms leaning onto the oak table. "When I was eight, my mother and I went for Easter service at a Catholic church."

"You went to church with your mother?" I interrupt, very curious.

Jack nods. "Yes, Mae, that day I went to church with my mother."

"You went to a Catholic church?" I ask, forgetting our guests and forgetting his waiting story.

Jack leans back in his chair, studying me, smiling at me. "Yes, Mae, I went to a Catholic church with my mother," he restates. "We went for Easter service, and there was a choir singing."

I can't help myself. "When did you stop going to church? When was the last time you saw your mother? I've never heard you mention your father."

Jack flicks his juice glass. It pings dully. He is glaring at me now. "Mae, let me finish, please. I just want to share a story."

I try hard to shut up.

"So there was this plump little boy in the front," Jack continues. "He still had chocolate on his face from his Easter basket breakfast. He was holding a hymnal in one hand and a toy truck in the other, a truck that he fiddled with the entire service. Most of the congregation was focused on that truck, too. The light kept catching it, and you could hear a quiet whirring when he played with the wheels. Even the priest was watching that truck, even during his sermon. When the priest called, 'Class Dismissed—'"

"Oh please, he doesn't say that."

Jack's eyes narrow. "Yes, Mae, I know."

I grow smug. I catch Oscar jumping on the sill, intently focused on the swaying cattails that poke up in my yard.

"When . . . service ended . . ." Jack says carefully, "The priest . . ." He stops, picking at his shirt pocket, visibly thinking. "You know, forget it. That story is pretty tame."

Jack laughs and begins again. I hear craziness in his throat and sense fearlessness in his mind. I worry. He turns to me and says, "Once I gave a girl head on church grounds."

Outside my window, the Huron River holds its breath.

"It's true," Jack says, looking at the water. "She was really turned on, and it was such a temperate summer night—calm, no bugs, a bright moon. We didn't want to waste such a night. So, I picked her up and laid her on the grass, about twenty feet from the double doors. She was a little uneasy at first, because the church has a glowing cross at night. She felt guilty, but I sure didn't."

My heart breaks. "Jack, when was this?"

"Last summer," he says, smiling snidely, knowing my response.

"While you were living here?"

"Yes, while I was living here."

I think about choices. I think about denominations. I think about traditions. I think about salvation and sin. I think about being twenty-two again, and I wonder how religion finds a person. I wonder what the ratio of believers to non-believers is based on those who were brought up with faith, those who weren't, and those who are drowning in guilt.

Remarkably, our breakfast guests aren't fazed, bless them. "So Mae, you must have some church stories to share. I bet you were pretty active in youth groups growing up, right?" Julie asks, sensing the need to ease my concerns.

I think about my youth. I try to recall a safe story to satisfy my friends. I wonder if sharing church stories is an appropriate memorial service for the Pope. I wonder how I let myself get this conflicted, given how much schooling I've endured. I want my friends to leave. I want Jack to leave. I want to lie down on the porch, with blankets and velvet pillows and a mug of strong coffee. I want to read and rest and enjoy my home in peace.

"Well, I do have a story," I say, happy to avenge Jack for making me upset. "I've tried to practice my faith, even though I shouldn't be allowed near a church," I state, eager for Jack's reaction. "And now I'm upset, because I thought this Pope was immortal. I've occasionally thought he was the next Christ. But it turns out, he was just human, he wasn't even magical, and his body is about to be paraded down the streets. So if he's not immortal, then surely I'm not immortal. This means that I will die one day, despite living a lot of my life like I never will. And if I'm not immortal, I'll have to be accountable for my actions. And while I guess I realized this a long time ago, I haven't changed anything. I still hurt people, and hurt myself. I'm still a bad person who did too much."

Sam and Julie look at the table. We've finally made them uncomfortable.

Jack leaves.

*

I awake to music notes drifting up the stairs and into my room. Jack is playing the clarinet, very softly, very smoothly. It sounds like a distant whale, his rich voice calling into the ocean. It is a familiar sound.

I took a nap after Sam and Julie left, their television safely in their arms. I apologized for my mood, for my difficulties, but they only smiled their warm smiles and said they'd see me soon.

Jack is playing a sonata. As I stand and pull on a sweater, I remember that Jack has a concert tonight. I step into my walk-in closet, flipping through dresses and jackets. The clarinet whale is growing louder. The clarinet whale is swimming my way. Jack is in my room now, walking toward the light of my closet. I see his shadow before I see him. He follows my invisible footsteps inside, stopping beside a shoe shelf. He plays as I continue to inspect dresses and jackets, scarves and belts. I creep toward the back, a focused marksman on my accessory hunt. He comes closer. His lips press hard, his breath and fingers creating playful scales and swollen low notes. He plays the clarinet like a piano, leaning in, leaning back, arching his shoulders. His notes grow short and quiet, and with his long bare foot, he kicks the closet door shut.

Trapped. "What are you doing?" I say, my hand clutching a bag from the cleaners.

He ignores me, breaking into a waltz, twirling 'round and 'round on my red Persian rug. I look above him at the little window in the closet, an octagon porthole-style window covered with wooden blinds. I could escape if I needed to. I could knock Jack unconscious with his clarinet, use his body as a step stool, and climb out the window and onto the roof.

I am unhealthy.

Jack stops. "This closet has the best acoustics in the house," he tells me. "Are you coming to my concert tonight?" he asks, brown eyes warm and kind.

"Did you lie about what you did to that girl?" I ask, my back touching the wall. Jack steps closer.

"No," he says, surprising me by sitting in the cramped room.

"Why are you sitting?"

"I'm tired," he says. "I had a strenuous afternoon."

"What did you do?"

"Took the boat out."

I find the window again. "Where did you take this girl?" I ask, avoiding his innocent face.

"St. Paul's."

I cringe, disgusted. I want to go to the church immediately and right this on Jack's behalf.

"Can I take you to dinner?" he asks, fingers creeping toward my foot.

I slip a blue dress off its hanger, draping it over my arm.

"You'd better," I say, my foot stepping on his spider hand.

"Wear a white dress," he tells me, held captive by my weight. "Fool me into thinking you're an angel."

*

I stand in the foyer of the concert hall, slowly moving forward behind the other patrons toward the auditorium and to my seat. We had a lovely dinner in town—glazed salmon and cold hoppy beer. The streets were enchanting tonight. There was a horse and buggy, students with lattes and croissants walking arm-in-arm, and gentlemen smoking fancy cigarettes and civilly talking about politics. There were distant night birds, and laughter from open bar doors, and whispers under street lamps. There were open-toed shoes and polo shirts. Spring really is a wonderful time, and really does deserve my anticipation each year.

I've been in this performance hall before, and I'm sure I'll be in it again. I've listened to Jack at work here on numerous occasions the past three years. The Brahms concert unfolds as expected. Jack does an excellent job as principal, the conductor is in lively form, and the orchestra makes no audible mistakes. I stand in my white dress during the ovation, raising my hands for Jack. He winks at me and I look away, hoping there aren't any colleagues in the hall tonight.

As we leave the building, the city has changed, the conversation is new. "He died an hour ago," I overhear. "The Pope finally died."

Jack snaps his head toward me, mouth agape. I nod blankly. "It's fine," I say. "I'm fine."

We get home just after eleven, clarinet case in his hand, and folded program in mine. The house looks different, somehow. It's like we've interrupted something. I'm cautious as I hang my coat. I peer around corners, look past furniture. "Jack, do you think someone's been here?"

He looks puzzled. "Like a burglar?"

I nod, shrug, wait for him to protect me.

"Well, your wallet is still where you left it." He points to the table. Oscar looks up from his couch nap, curiously blinking.

"I guess it's just me," I say, retreating up the stairs. But I'm shaking as I push open my bedroom door.

Nothing. Paranoia is an unwelcome houseguest.

Soon I'm in my bed. I spend so much time asleep in spurts throughout the day, a wasted life in many respects. I alter my schedule to fit in naps, think about sleep repeatedly during my alert hours. I can't wait to get into bed, and yet, I'm most lonesome and uncomfortable in bed. It's not long before I'm too restless to continue trying for sleep, and so I head downstairs with a task in mind.

I grab a tape measure from the back porch and flip on the chandelier light in the dining room. Everything looks so artificially orange as I work while the sun is on the other side of the earth, making me feel a little sick as I measure the width of the chest of drawers, then each individual drawer to assess its capacity. I scribble numbers on a legal pad and forecast that I have about four more years before I run out of space. I also decide I must find a way to lock it all up, which will be hard to do without involving someone else since I'm no good with my hands.

Back upstairs, I do sleep for a stretch, waking up before sunrise. I feel another urge to go to St. Paul's. Determined, I throw back the covers and slip on sneakers without socks.

I poke my head into the hallway. I have to pass Jack's room to get out of the house. I swear Jack sometimes sleeps with one eye open. Jack is my keeper, my guard. Jack is also a whistleblower, warning me when my behavior scares him. Panicked, I slink away from the door and shuffle into the closet. Wooden beams from the porthole window glow. I stack boxes of financial paperwork that were against the back wall and stand on my new platform. I unhook the window's gold latch and pull myself through the opening and into the night. My God, all these years, and all that was preventing a rapist from attacking me was a small gold latch. Seconds later, my feet are on the roof, stepping over leaves that are on their way to the gutters.

*

In his room, Jack watches his ceiling tremble, human footsteps jarring him from dreams. He'll give Mae a head start.

CHAPTER 4

I pull on St. Paul's door. The code failed, and I stare at the lock perplexed, studying the unit with growing frustration. Glances over both shoulders confirm that I'm alone. The parking lot is sleeping in the spring mist, dusted with flower parts and grass shards. Air swirls in my mouth. It's going to be a humid day.

I touch my forehead to the door's window, squinting tightly. The altar is nothing but a box, a simple square in the back of the room. The pews look like logs. The sanctuary is a graveyard of objects. Frustrated, I jog to the side door. The numbers fall off my fingers and the lock gives a hopeful click. I grab the door's handle and twist. Nothing. I run to the back, crunching gravel and twigs and acorns. There is a low window. I squat, pushing and pulling the pane. I grunt and wince and fail to get inside St. Paul's. On the edge of the earth, I see the first hue of the day, slowly spreading like watercolor. Defeated, I tug my hair and leave.

I pass a row of identical church windows as I walk. They mock me, laughing at my ineptness. I raise my arm, letting my fingers glide over glass and brick, glass and brick as I start for home. At the last window, I stop. It's a building, a structure. I pull my sweatshirt over my head, the University of Michigan's logo disappearing as I wrap it around my fist. I tap the glass with my bare hand. It's thick, and textured. It's definitely going to hurt.

Channeling Jack's strength, I clench my jaw and prepare to punch.

*

In Mae's front yard, Jack is crawling on his hands and knees. He peers under bushes, into flower beds, and behind the fake windmill. Standing up, he slinks along the wall, stopping to listen as he makes his way south. Oscar is watching Jack approach, the cat interested and playful. Tiptoeing under Oscar, Jack rounds the corner to the backyard.

He steps onto the pier, sunlight turning into a spotlight. He watches Mae's house, dark and peaceful. The houses on the far side of the water are dark and peaceful, too. Mae said she'd like to rebuild the pier this year, as it's showing a lot of wear. "There could be an accident," she said. "I don't want anyone getting hurt."

Jack crouches on the rotting planks, untying the boat from the dock. He can watch the house better from the water. He can wait and see exactly when Mae comes home.

*

I take the long way back, with my sweatshirt on again. I didn't do it. I didn't break into St. Paul's. I realized that there are other churches, other days, other matters to tend to.

I turn the key quietly, push the door open slowly. I step into the living room and lock the door behind me. My ferns are wilting and my magazines are piling up. My floor needs sweeping and my sills are getting dusty. Perhaps I'll clean today.

I climb the stairs, but stop when I notice Jack's door is ajar. My eyes scan his empty room, stopping on his alarm clock. It's just before seven in the morning. Where has Jack gone at this hour? Maybe he's gone looking for me. I thump down the hall, no longer concerned about keeping things at a hush. From my bedroom, I can see a view of most of the neighborhood. My room is so much more exposed than the rest of the rooms. I am Rapunzel in her tower, watching and waiting. Through the glass I see sloping roofs and fluffy trees. I see sturdy mailboxes and black driveways. No sign of Jack. I leave my room and cross the hall to my bathroom, snapping open the blinds. I see my backyard, trimmed and elegant from Jack's upkeep. I see the water, waves rhythmically lapping in one direction. No sign of Jack. No sign of my boat, either.

The sun grows fierce and my tension grows, too. He's been taking my boat out a lot lately. I'm glad someone is making use of my father's old boat, but no inexperienced handler should go out alone. Especially a young man, with eager hands and big ideas. I have a feeling he anchors frequently to explore shorelines which must bother the neighbors. I'm certain some normal boat activity is involved. He probably fishes for a while, throwing back everything that bites the line since I've never seen him bring anything back. But who's to say what else happens in that boat. I know he's taken girls out there. I know he's stayed out all night before. Jack may be the smartest kid I know, and he may be the most resourceful, but he's still under my watch and he's still dangerous. I know Jack thinks it's the other way around, that I'm his to look after. But he's the jobless one, he's the feisty one, he's the impassioned one. Jack doesn't have to try hard—there is plenty of trouble for Jack to get into easily. Trouble finds young able guys like Jack.

I'm supposed to be working. I should be doing something. But as I sit in my kitchen, fiddling with napkin rings and staring into empty corners, I can only think of Jack, somewhere in my father's old boat that I moved over to this house, and how my dependence and concern over Jack has made me unable to do anything. Our codependent relationship is too limiting.

I hear a familiar smack and see the screen door shake. My weekend edition of *The Ann Arbor Times* is here. I slide back from the table, from my thoughts, and patter through the warm living room to the porch. The paperboy is standing on my sidewalk, gaunt and sullen, with an eyebrow piercing that resembles a sewing needle. I smile politely and scoop up my paper.

"Your subscription is almost up, Ms. Harrington."

"Can I mail a check to the office?" I ask, feeling strange with this kid waiting on me. He replies, "Sure," hands deep in his pockets.

"There aren't any clouds today," he says, looking straight ahead. He rounds his back, his shoulders caving in. He is a gargoyle, or some kind of demon, perched on my walk, ready to greet visitors like a gothic statue. His face turns, wings shifting behind him as he meets my eyes. I drop my stare, fearfully focused on his feet, watching for a tail to curl around his toes.

"Have you been to Nora Park lately?" he asks. "You live very close to Nora Park."

I was at the park last week. I like to walk to Nora Park to watch the night fishermen, their lit bobbers dancing madly and their flashlight beams crossing paths. I like to see the guys sit on their dirty pails, laughing and chewing tobacco, eating sandwiches with dirty hands. Meanwhile, the city sleeps behind them, dimly glowing and calmly waiting until morning to live again.

"I haven't gone there in awhile," I say, scared that the gargoyle is more perceptive than he lets on.

"That's probably good," he says, "because I have something to tell you about Nora Park." I squeeze my newspaper, my whole arm tight with dread.

"What's that?" I ask.

He pulls his satchel over his head, apparently ready to return to delivering. "A girl drowned there last night. So maybe you should stay away from that place."

The gargoyle crouches and leaves on all fours, putting claw marks in the cement.

*

Jack is bewildered. "He said a girl drowned there?" he asks, with windblown hair and pink cheeks. I nod. "Did you look at the paper? Is there a story?"

I shake my head, amazed that I hadn't thought to read the paper. Jack says, "Stay here," and leaves to fetch today's edition. He returns a moment later, his head hidden behind the headlines. "I don't see anything," he says, snapping pages open and closed. "Mae, we need to buy a television. We really do. Or hey, at least try to live in this decade and maybe turn on your computer for news instead of waiting on the town rumor mill?"

I stand, sufficiently scared and ready to admit that we should have better access to live news. "Let me change," I say, "and we'll take a drive."

Jack follows close behind. "Aren't you going to church this morning?" he asks.

"No," I tell him. "I was just there this—"

I stop. Jack walks into my back, his hands grabbing my shoulders. "You were just there this . . . ?" he asks, his breath warm on my ear.

"I was just there this week," I say, trying to sound nonchalant. His hands fall down my arms, and I start walking again. I go up the stairs while he waits at the bottom. I exhale in my bedroom, worried over how close I came to slipping.

I return to him, and once in the car Jack drives away from the river. He tells me, "There used to be this great little place out this way. I don't know if it's still open. Hope so."

Road construction is heavy, as it always is between snow months, with horns and break lights pulsing. Soon fields replace machines, and I catch a glimpse of a trailer park set back from the road, set down among nice sturdy trees.

We pull into an electronics store near railroad tracks, which are so old and delicate looking that I wonder if the tracks used to carry the merchandise right into this out-of-the-way place. Hundreds of Pope heads dance on television screens inside. John Paul II is wearing purple, then red, then white.

"When is his burial?" I ask Jack.

"Not for a few days. It takes time for important people to get to Rome."

We walk single file, squeezed by John Paul II who is now shaking the president's hand. I round the corner to the back, where projection screens make the Pope's body larger than my own. "How big of a television do we need?" I ask.

Jack points to the corner. "That will do."

A clerk rings up our new thirty-two inch flat screen. He swipes my credit card and tells me I have thirty days for an exchange or return. We thank him and Jack carries our purchase to my car, where the box fits snugly in my trunk.

Jack stands outside the car, looking across the road at something I'm not seeing. "Mind if we take a little detour before we go home?" he says. "There's this campground I like just a few minutes away." I shrug and settle into the car with the television manual.

"Are we going to need an antenna since I don't have cable?" I ask, eyes scanning all the technical charts. I don't even look up from my manual until Jack turns the car off, right next to a droopy swing set, which is in a rusty little park inside a sleepy-looking campground.

I slide out of my seat and watch Jack, hands in his pockets, his feet making a dark wet path as he walks across dewy grass. He stops at an old, dented metal slide, leaning against it and having a real good look around. "Did you camp here growing up?" I ask him.

Jack shakes his head no. He nods up toward a wooden sign overhead, shaped like an arch for the cars to drive under. *Hidden Trails Campground*, it reads, slightly swaying near what I think is an owl's nest. It's all very rustic and intangibly inviting, like a '50s postcard. I wonder what Jack knows about this place, but I'm anxious to get home. I stand, as patiently as possible, while Jack makes slow turns, looking this way and that way.

"Can we take a quick picture under the sign?" he asks, setting up a little digital camera I didn't know he had on top of the slide. It starts to beep and Jack trots up to me, throwing an arm over my shoulder for the photo. We smile as the flash goes, and he scurries back to retrieve the camera as I open the car door. "Thanks," he says, getting behind the wheel.

I look around as we drive out, up a long steep driveway, probably great for sledding. The road is made from dirt, the light tan kind that makes enormous puffy clouds behind you as your tires roll over. We're seemingly just on a drive through the woods until an abandoned swimming pool comes into view, the deep end full of concrete chunks and surrounded by a sagging metal fence. A red wooden store sits near the pool, with firewood piled up on all sides. The place is boarded up and has definitely seen better days. Jack turns beside it, staring at it out my window as we crawl past. I study his eyes, which are definitely recalling something. Soon he cuts across to an outlet road and we're back on the highway headed toward Ann Arbor. "Let's go pick up an antenna now," he decides. "Yes, you need one."

We drive to a large hardware store not far from my house, where ladders and shovels and bird feeders are propped up outside against the building. Inside, couples inspect paint colors, widows compare home security systems, and college roommates laugh at cheeky doormats. Jack talks to a clerk, describing our roof and options. Sixty dollars later, Jack is satisfied.

"Jack," I say, wild with confusion. "Did you just pay for that?"

"Yeah," he says, looking at me oddly.

"How do you pay your rent each month? How are you paying for school? Where did that nice camera come from?" I just realized, after years of living with him, that Jack has never brought up money. This is highly unusual for a college student, especially one who doesn't even work after class.

"I got a bunch of money my Dad set aside for me. Got to pick it up when I turned eighteen."

"Oh . . . oh Jack, I didn't know your father died. You've never really talked about—"

"I didn't say he was dead." And by his sharp tone, I know I can say no more, though I was about to reveal a thing or two we have in common, big things, right here in this noisy store.

We take a back road home, hoping to avoid church traffic. I drive. A tractor is in front of us, its open-top trailer heaped with fresh corn. Green husks are flying madly off the top, some spinning to the pavement, others picked up by the wind and hurled into neighboring fields. A few husks crash into my windshield, getting stuck under the wipers like unwanted advertisements. "Shit, this is dangerous," Jack says, his voice a bit squeaky. "We have some deviant agricultural behavior here." I snicker, relieved to hear that he can still joke around after our abrupt earlier conversation, until I remember the gargoyle. I only told Jack about the drowning; I left out the part about the paperboy turning into a creature.

Somberness covers me slowly.

"Hey," Jack says, breaking my trance. "It'll be summer soon. Maybe we can go somewhere." His eyes grow wide, childlike. "Maybe we could take the boat through the locks, Mae. We could try to boat right over to Canada! Do you think we could find enough connecting waterways?" Strangely, I've never been to Canada, even though it's so close. I feel Jack's energy and get excited.

"Or hey!" he says, his body straining against the seatbelt. "We could go to California! I've never been to California. You could show me around." We cross over a wooden bridge, familiar with its big elegant posts rising up over a commonplace Michigan lake. Bridges and lakes like this, they're everywhere in the Midwest. The bridges are steel for highways, but on the edges of town they're always wood.

Then corncobs pelt the car, denting the metal down to nothing. We're buried under yellow lines and asphalt, but at least we stayed out of the water. Above us, cars whir by, unable to see the new coffins.

"Mae!" Jack shouts, invading my nightmare. "Mae, you almost drove off the road!" I snap back, aware of my body, aware of our vehicle, aware of the corn truck. Jack is pale and terrified, his childlike excitement but a memory. For minutes, we don't speak.

I keep driving, finally talking about the corncobs hitting us, and Jack stares. Then he says, "Where do you go?"

I blink. I shake my head, confused at his question.

"Where do you go when you don't want to hear something?" he asks, his voice timid.

"I don't know what you're talking about."

"I said, 'California,' and you left this car when we drove over that bridge," Jack says. "Your mind completely left this car."

We pass the *Welcome to Ann Arbor* sign. This is the least attractive way to enter town. On our right, a few ugly houses sit alone, barred from being any closer to downtown. Overhead, a 747 coughs and roars, sailing up from Detroit. When I was getting ready to move to Ann Arbor, everyone told me how hard I was going to fall in love. "There are so many trees, so much smart energy," they said. "The university culture is great, and the city is so active, so engaged." I saw that immediately. I did. But geography is tricky with me. Unless I can convince everyone I've ever known to come to the same place, I'll always feel like I'm missing something; like maybe they're all talking poorly about me somewhere and I can't keep tabs on the conversation. Like a part of my story is continuing without me. I'm glad Jack is here. I'm glad I found Julie and Sam here. I'm certainly glad I'm here, but still, it's not quite right.

We arrive home. Jack keeps looking me up and down like I'm new to earth. So I take to studying my favorite picture—that famous picture of half the earth taken from space, with all that black around us, and the brilliant blue and white swirls of our planet. I get overwhelmed when I hold this picture. It's incredible. And it's kind of like true cooperative globalization—no borders, no ideologies, just us. It's almost eerie how beautiful we look from above. This picture would never have been taken if I were the astronaut holding the camera. My hands would have shook too much to press the trigger. My eyes would have watered too much to focus the frame. And frankly, if it worked out, I wouldn't have shared it with anybody back home because I'd selfishly want it for myself, so therefore, it would never really exist.

The phone rings in the kitchen. I hear Jack mumbling. And then quite clearly he says, "I just told you, she isn't here." A moment later he passes by, surely en route to his room for his daily *active meditation* ritual that he's taken up, convinced he's found a new kind of mind relaxer or Tai Chi to make him famous.

But I'm curious. "Who wanted to talk to me?" I ask.

*

Jack doesn't answer. Instead, he closes his door and thinks about Mae. He watched her come home early this morning, looking strange and wild as she slipped through the front door. He took a boat ride down the river to think things through, recounting all of Mae's psychotic episodes. When Mae mentioned the paperboy later, and the drowning, he had another episode to file away. And still another in the car when she all but killed the two of them before she snapped out of whatever cloud she was under. The case for putting her into a treatment program is growing daily, but Jack knows he can't be without her, even for one single day. And now, some ex-boyfriend named Brian is trying to reach her.

He decides Mae is too unstable to know about this.

*

It's Monday morning now, and I'm expected in the classroom in a little over an hour. Jack was awake and gone before me, though he does have an eight o'clock music theory class. He never misses a class, and always studies extra hard for exams. Strange, he'll be graduating in less than a week, and all of this routine business will be done.

I carefully arrange my day into my briefcase: graded papers for my first class, notes for the student advisory committee meeting, and a final lecture for my second class before I hand out the last exam. Today is busy, but not hectic. I have office hours as well, but office hours are pretty sleepy on Mondays. I may get a hysterical student or two, worried about their last test and where they stand, but I'll have plenty of time to just sit and be, thinking of the rest of the week, tired already.

I'm on campus and in my building within twenty minutes of leaving my house, and I parked very far away today. I sometimes long for big city living, but enjoy the conveniences of a smaller city. More often I long to live alone, in the country, on a small hobby farm with chickens and berries. I'd be at peace. I wouldn't be so distracted by who is doing what or who is missing from my life. Oscar would be happy, content to hunt in the tall weeds until the sun went down and the moon rose, dew forming under his paws. I guess Ann Arbor provides a close compromise, since all of that is just a short car ride away.

As I turn the corner to my classroom, I see students ducking inside, holding their notebooks in hand. I decide to stop at my faculty mailbox in case another announcement came over the weekend. The Dean took us all sorts of places this semester: pay freezes, required staff reviews, less funding for our graduate students. A typical public university onslaught, perhaps, though more dismal news than usual.

Today a single paper awaits me, with a headline declaring: "Student Honorees Named." Below, a list of the top students from each area is listed, with an invitation for their professors to join these students at the awards ceremony at the end of the week. I scan the names, not knowing a soul. None of my students; not this year, not last year, oh well. And then I gasp in recognition: "Jack Mekinski, School of Music."

Jack.

I am excited, elated, eager to know if he's aware of this. What a gift he has, with music, with knowledge. I float into my classroom and take my place behind the podium. Today we are covering Chaucer's *The Canterbury Tales*. As usual, the classroom is mostly arranged by aptitude, a well-known layout by instructors and students alike. The hardest working are early, and in the front, pens poised and coffee steaming. Some of the achievers are sprinkled in the middle too, because they were running a little late today. And as expected, the frat boys with red eyes and scruffy chins are in the back, as are the academically insecure, who'd rather blend into the background. A church congregation, a classroom, both arranged to my expectations on most days, with one large exception: Jack always sits in the back.

A few minutes into my lecture on the role of Middle English and I'm already with Jack, thinking about his upcoming award. Will he tell his mother, I wonder? They talk so rarely, and I really don't know when he last visited her, despite telling me that she's in Michigan. Bigger still, will his mother come to the graduation ceremony? Surely she knows he's graduating this year. Surely she knows this is the end of the line and is wondering where he'll go next . . .

. . . a sea of heads snap up as my chalk breaks in half. I push myself forward, continue my lecture the best I can.

I can't believe I don't know where Jack is going next.

*

During office hours, I finally let myself return to the real matter at hand. I flew on autopilot this morning, had a multitasking kind of lunch that kept my head from overthinking, and now I'm seated, and really thinking. There's a small maple tree outside my window. The grounds crew planted it a few years back. I didn't care much for trees until I became a homeowner. Watching vulnerable life take root and try to make it is so inspiring, so delicate. I feel such accomplishment when my perennials come back in their soft beds, so sad when some die away for good. I think this maple has a good shot of being a campus landmark one day. It's growing faster than I expected, and is already drawing artists and poets. I watch them sketch out leafy branches, write expected prose about strength and growing up. Will I still be around when this tree is full-grown, I wonder? Will they put a fountain around it, or a bench underneath for daydreaming?

A crisp knock echoes across my office. I turn and meet Jack's gaze. He is concerned. And, somehow, looking a little nervous, which is rather unlike Jack.

He reaches behind to pull out a folded piece of paper from his back pocket. "Did you see this?" he asks, still looking concerned, still looking nervous.

He places the awards list on my desk, spinning it my direction. "I did, Jack," I say. "I'm so proud of you. This is big."

He smiles strangely, playing with his hands. "Thanks. So I was just wondering, if you'd be my date on Thursday."

I laugh. "I can't be your date."

Jack scratches his hands. "I mean, you don't have to wear a shirt announcing it. I just thought we could get dinner before, maybe a drink after."

I shift my weight. "It'd be risky, showing up to a campus event. I'm pretty sure no one knows you live with me."

Jack nods, eyes cast downward.

"I suppose you'd want me to take your arm and everything," I say, a little too flip for his condition.

He changes. "If you're so concerned about being seen with a student, why did you rent a room to a student?" he says strongly. We've both thought about this, I'm certain, but we've never voiced it.

"It just seemed easy," I say.

"Well, I suppose you're not stuck with me for much longer."

Anxiety spreads like new tree roots across my chest. I do my best to sound calm, sound interested. "What are your summer plans?" I ask plainly. I'm so insecure about my life; I never knew just how much until Jack's presence brought it to my attention.

He tips his head, looks at me with his incredible eyes, his lips pushing down at the corners. He is sad. "I should leave you," he says.

CHAPTER 5

January 7, 1995.

Southern California welcomed me with El Niño and startling earthquakes within moments of arriving from Minnesota. But she also hooked me up with another Midwest transplant, who is currently buttoning his Sunday best while I remain under the sheets. He's the baritone section leader at a nearby Presbyterian power church, a gig that pays $150 a week, which is just enough to make his college student life a bit smoother. I hear the intercom and I know it's Nora, the soprano section leader, coming to get a ride with Brian. "Come up," he says, and I sit up to protest.

"Hey, I'm not even dressed."

Brian looks at me smugly, strangely. "Hasn't she seen you in less?" he says evenly, in the kind of way a kid with a lot of uneven nights shouldn't be saying. These little barbs flick out lately, sharpened from his insomnia. I thought winter break back in Kansas would gently cradle him back into that pleasant, wide-eyed boy with a love for salt water that I met when I backed my SUV into his flimsy Civic. But he returned from break in worse shape, nearly deranged in fact, saying vague but severe complaints like, "I can't take this anymore," while refusing to elaborate to me or anyone.

The door clicks open and Nora's clean face smiles in the

doorframe. "Is everyone appropriate?" she wants to know in her cute Euro accent. She's tiny, and blonde, but commanding and fascinating. When I kissed her cheeks on New Year's, when all those people were drunk and partying here in this now communal apartment, I remembered thinking she was the kind of captivating person whom I'd never get out of my head, a year from now, a lifetime from now. No one could. Not with her beautiful hair like marbled glass, with her kindness as lovely and clear as Christmas snow. I don't know much about her life, but I feel like everyone knows this Nora.

Brian fills up his water bottle and nods in my direction. "Can we bring you back lunch?" he wants to know. I decline, he blows a kiss, and I hear his keys jingle down the hall.

Nora lingers. "I need to talk to you this afternoon," she whispers, then follows Brian's sounds away from this apartment and through the gates of St. Cecilia's, singing in harmony to a congregation of two thousand.

*

I'm sitting in an uneven chair, slowly rocking the metal back and forth, clink and clank. We're outside the café in sweaters, the place between our apartments, under an umbrella protecting us from drippy sky sprinkles. Nora is circling verses in her Bible with a red felt pen. "Do you feel guilty about defacing a Bible?" I ask her while I open a sugar packet for my coffee.

She gives me an odd look. "It's just a printing, this book," she says. "It isn't sacred. Or were you kidding?" She seems so concerned about my question that I answer, "Yeah, I was just trying to rouse you." Though sincerely, I feel that she's defacing a sacred text and that she should knock it off. A red felt pen no less, bleeding through all that onion skin paper.

I can almost see the mountains behind downtown today, which

is always a notable day in Los Angeles. I'm thinking about the last time I saw the mountains when she says, "So about that boyfriend of yours . . . we have to figure out what the heck is wrong with him."

When we started dating, I sent his picture back to Minnesota to a high school friend, all nerves and euphoria. "He's a little young, isn't he?" she replied. Now I can't see anything else: he's a year older than me, but his narrow face, his lithe body, his small hands, they are not. It's like he's growing differently than the rest of us, like he's just getting started. Maybe emotionally, too.

"He's just so insanely moody, like a broad who doesn't get her way, you know?" Nora says. I see this side of him, but I also feel his protection, his interest in my interests, hear his squeaky laugh, so I don't really care if he's up and down. All college students are up and down, I convince myself.

The café's radio starts pumping the latest Counting Crows hit indoors and out, and I gaze across the street at a group of black-haired kids playing soccer. It's so nice to just sit and chat, but somehow, meeting up with a girlfriend for afternoon coffee is always an undertaking. Small talk always grows into big whales, who sweep their giant tails in and out of the conversation.

"Brian's getting worse all the time. And he's not sleeping, you know. At least not much, maybe in short spurts here and there. He's definitely tired enough to sleep, and I thought he might just nod off on our drive to church this morning, but he won't let himself sleep. It's like he's afraid to sleep," she concludes.

This gives me pause, and I stop to examine the pebbly cement under my chair. Last night when I slept over, I woke up twice from noises, from sounds. The first time he was at his desk, typing, just a glowing outline across the room. The second time, his fingernails were scratching at the headboard, just above my bangs. In my dream it was a cat, trying to come in from outside. After I woke and saw it was Brian, his eyes glazed and fixed into a corner, I couldn't sleep, either. I wanted to comfort him, but I knew he was too upset, too tired, too distracted in a way that I cannot comprehend nor help.

"Maybe it's just stress," she offers. "He does have that audition in an hour."

"What audition?" I snap, rapt with attention. "Where?"

Nora's mouth falls open slightly and she scrunches her eyebrows. "Brian didn't mention it? He's auditioning for a role with the L.A. Opera. Not a lead or anything, but a pretty big deal considering he doesn't have much professional experience. He's been really freaked out about it. Really, he hasn't mentioned it?"

My chair shrieks as it scrapes the pebbly foundation below, and I rise at once. "I want to go hear him."

"It's not an open audition," Nora says. "Sit down, I want to know how you spent your break back home, Mae. How was Minnesota?"

But I am up and moving, my hands feeling for my purse, my keys, that little repaired hole at the end of my pocket that Brian hand-sewed during a different sleepless night. "Another time, then?" Nora calls out to me as I wave goodbye.

"I didn't go home," I shout back to her. "I stayed here, in Los Angeles. Just by myself."

Nora remains seated, confused and flustered from Mae's sudden departure, her hand smoothing a Bible page. She didn't go home for Christmas? Does Brian know? Do these two even talk to each other anymore?

*

I don't hear anything at first as I slip into the auditorium through the back by the sound equipment. Down below, rows away, a few men and women sit in everyday clothes, holding clipboards with lights attached. At the back of the stage, instead of the usual piano accompanying solo auditions, a few percussion players are staggered around.

There is a shiny timpani, fat and stout, sitting on an elevated platform. The player, fairly fat and stout himself, stands snugly between the drums, carefully tapping away with giant matchstick mallets. He bends close, listening to the pitches. No one is singing, no one else is even preparing, but there he stands, compulsively listening, compulsively tuning. After moments—minutes even—frowns, and scowls, he finally stands erect and declares, "I'm ready. Next vocalist, please." Between the exacting standards rolling out on stage and the vast, empty auditorium before him, I'm sure Brian is shaking backstage. I almost wish he could see me up here, the girlfriend who snuck in to see him, though I know I'm best kept in the dark.

But if he is scared, he isn't going to let anyone know, not even himself. Brian enters the stage in a tuxedo, with slicked-back hair, and a wide and warm smile befitting a boy from Kansas. He's far away, but I can recognize the sparkle of the cuff links I bought him last month. He looks genuinely happy, earnestly excited, maybe with a touch of swagger, too. My fear for him evaporates as he adjusts the front microphone. It's like he's the judge, like he's welcoming the others to this audition. The way he can flip on such confidence reassures me he's in the right profession, and this is the right chance for a Midwestern guy with everything to gain out here on the sunny coast.

He sings, and I am his.

*

I visit Brian at bedtime, where we eat a nice late supper under his fake down comforter. He doesn't know that I was at his audition, and I want to figure out why he's been hiding this from me. "How was your day?" I ask, lounging in his pajama pants beside him, my thin tank top pressed against his chest. I'm calm, and perfectly ordinary. I will not accuse him of anything, especially with his recent bouts of fragility and unease.

"It was alright. Sang with Nora. Had stuff to do downtown this afternoon."

Now I'm disappointed, but I hide it, for him. I feel like I've got to be extra careful and perfect to keep him, because he is special and talented, and I'm am less so. He has options, and I haven't many. I'm good at studying and thinking critically. I'm pretty, but not outrageously so. I can make decent casseroles. He is a star, and I am not. Someday I hope I'll be more confident, but for now, on this Sunday and every Sunday since, I'm still growing into myself.

I sit up and feather his hair between my hands. I hear his breathing slow, and I know he's finally relaxing. His belly is full, and now maybe I can empty his mind for sleep. I slide my hands to his shoulders to give him a massage. He's really relaxing now. Without thinking I start to sing, this rusty-sounding folk song that I always sing in my head to put myself to sleep. It makes me think of traveling and of good people. I get softer and softer, bringing it to a lullaby level, when I turn self-conscious and the notes taper off.

Brian's eyes flutter open. "Why did you stop? It was so beautiful. You sound so beautiful. I love your voice."

My heart swells but my mind hurts. I want to ask him to tell me everything, and to demand more from me: to make me help him. I want to be useful and needed. But for tonight, maybe I can just get him to sleep. I start to sing again, in his darkened room with only our outlines visible. His breathing changes again, and after a few minutes, I know he's gone under. I change my song to a whisper, the song about orange summers and picnics on piers, as he goes further away beside me. I stop, listening to the familiar sounds of his room, and to the intermittent traffic horns or distant helicopter hovering.

Brian is asleep now. As I continue to listen to the world past his apartment, I know Los Angeles is starting to go to sleep now, too, preparing for another week of office work, movie sets, and fishing on the sea. Within the hour, I've quietly gathered my things and slipped out of his apartment, heading down the path between the shops to my own place.

*

Brian wakes violently shortly after Mae leaves. He's sweating and confused. "I've got to get her out of the water," he says, throwing the covers to the floor with a desperateness he's unwilling to confront.

*

I am miserable. This week, one of the longest of my life, was spent with a fussy clarinet player who is too smart for his own good. Jack is unhappy, so I am unhappy. Classes are a chore this week for both of us, even though I just have to administer exams. But I suppose with the continually warming temperatures, and everyone's mind on graduation, no one is noticing our weak performances: me, the teacher; him, the student. I often remind myself that this is indeed our relationship, but my confidence in our arrangement never lasts long. Jack is never satisfied with me, and my mind grows continually sicker.

It's Wednesday evening, the night before his award ceremony. After much resistance from Jack, I finally pressured him into calling his mother with the help of warm apple strudel for a reward. His mother, probably startled to hear from him, confessed she wasn't really prepared to go to a formal event on such short notice (as reported by Jack), but asked if it'd be alright if she stayed here

the night before his graduation to attend the commencement ceremonies. Jack relayed all of this to me after he hung up; I was
hoping to eavesdrop on the conversation with this mystery mom,
but he wandered out back while on the phone. But finally, after
three years, I'll get to shake her hand. And, strangely enough, I'll
get to make her bed.

Oscar strolls by my legs and reports to the back door to go outside. Jack and I get up in unison. Jack stops short. I continue on
and let Oscar out onto the deck, where he immediately lies down
and takes to rolling across the pine planks. The air is so sweet and
mixed, smelling of irises and algae from the river. I look over my
sloping lawn and at my pier. It looks more unstable each year.
"Jack," I call. In a moment, he is with me.

"We should really fix the pier this summer, don't you think? It's
getting dangerous."

And as soon as the words are out, I remember that Jack wants
to leave this summer. I swallow the knot away in my throat. He's
graduating. He's twenty-two. He should leave. He should travel,
or work, or start graduate school somewhere new. He'll succeed
wherever he goes, but I know that he should definitely go.

"I forgot, you're almost out of here," I tell him, as Oscar ventures off the deck and onto the lawn. I hear Jack breathing. I sense
the distance between our breaths shortening, our air mixing together.

"Actually, I'm glad you mentioned the pier. I was just on it the
other day, and you're right, we really need to fix it soon," he says.
"I'll stay until it's done."

We look over my property together. Jack did a lot around here
the past three years. He's good about helping with the gardening
and fall cleanup. My yard is so colorful now, so carefully plotted
now. He's good with his hands. He has a good work ethic. But

moreover, he's just good at what he does, whatever he does, except love.

"Jack, do you want me to write you a letter of recommendation? For grad school, or for work?" I ask. "That's a customary request this time of year."

The phone trills in the house. I step inside while Jack remains on the deck thinking over my offer. I turn the oven on as I walk into the kitchen, already looking forward to our roasted chicken tonight. It's so pleasant to cook for someone. I'll really miss it.

"Hello," I say, reaching for the spice jars overhead.

"Mae," he says.

And just like that, my life changes.

". . . Brian? Is that you?" I ask, certain that it is. I am instantly sweaty, instantly pained.

"Yeah, it's me. I tried to reach you the other night, but your husband said you were out."

My husband. Jack. And Brian, calling me. I am overwhelmed. I am dizzy. I'm back in college now, riding on his handlebars, off to the late show. "I'm not married. You spoke to my tenant. Why are you calling me?"

"You're not married, Mae?"

"Why are you calling me?" I look out the kitchen window, where Jack is roaming the yard collecting sticks. He's probably going to mow. "What is this about?" I feel so terrible, so instantly terrible.

I hear Brian inhale. He exhales without speaking. Soon, he says, "I need to see you. I want to tell you some things."

I'm watching Jack now. He's dragging the mower out of my shed.

"When did you try calling me?" I ask.

"Sunday evening," Brian says. Jack is revving the motor now. Oscar slinks under the deck, fearful of the noise.

I was definitely home on Sunday evening.

"Just tell me whatever it is you need to tell me right now," I say, sounding strong, sounding sure. I have many memories of us; after twelve idle years, I still like a few, but hate most.

"I'd rather just see you. I think I should tell you in person."

Jack is mowing now, making beautifully straight lines of green and deeper green leading up to the water.

"Where do you live these days?" I ask.

"About three hours away."

Three hours! Twelve years, and three hours away. Jack stops to move a garden rock. He is purposeful, and efficient. I want to make him proud of me. I want to thank him for all that he's done for me. And now, perhaps I can.

"No, Brian. And please don't call me again."

Twelve years of forgetting, one minute to remember.

*

Once again, I'm in my closet. And once again, a clarinet whale is swimming my way. But I can't be trapped tonight, can't let him know what I'm up to. I step out of the closet and into my bedroom, pulling out the chair in front of my bureau. I take to organizing my earrings while the whale swims up the stairs, his big, slow tail propelling him toward me. The whale is in my room now, krill exploding from his keys. When he reaches me, Jack lowers his clarinet.

He's standing in a dress shirt and tie with nicely pressed slacks. He's about to leave for his award ceremony. Tonight is Thursday. Just three days until graduation.

"I'm heading out now. I'll be home in a few hours."

I nod. "I'll be waiting to hear all about it," I say, smiling in a polite matronly way.

Jack leaves. After the front door closes, I dash back into the closet and pull out a sundress and cardigan. Moments later, I'm in my car and heading toward campus, just a few minutes behind Jack.

Parking is easy. Campus is never empty, but it's certainly quiet tonight. Lots of studying silhouettes in the library windows, and more are packing the outlying coffee shops to prepare for their last finals tomorrow. I walk through the sidewalk and shrub mazes to Angell Auditorium. Students are walking in with their parents, with their professors. I merge into the crowd. Everyone is happy, everyone is proud. I wonder if Jack feels either.

Once inside, I tuck myself away into the furthest corner. There are plenty of colleagues around. Some spot me and smile. I haven't done anything wrong, I remind myself; we don't roll around together. I reach down into my handbag and pull out my camera. This is just for Jack. This is to show my support, and to capture this moment for him. Maybe someday, when he's less dramatic and moody, he'll hold the photo I took of him and feel simple warmth, easy joy. Perhaps he'll want to share the photo with his mother when she visits.

Brian's call is eating away at me, and my mind flips between sitting in this auditorium, waiting to see Jack's big moment, and remembering sitting in auditoriums listening to Brian sing solos. I've considered all extremes for his call, but find some peace in knowing that if this pushes me to madness, I can always meet up with him and get it over with. He's not dead; in fact, he's remarkably close. Just an afternoon's drive away. And I'm intensely glad that I don't know which direction to drive to meet him, for temptation grows as the hours pass.

The Dean approaches the podium and the crowd's murmur fizzles into silence. "Good evening," she says. "Thank you for being here on this wonderful night to celebrate our students' achievements."

She makes generalizations about good students for a few minutes. She then transitions into generalizations about our good university, and our good professors, sprinkling in witty anecdotes along the way. She is articulate, she is commanding. She waits for the perfect amount of time after chuckles float up from the seats and looks comfortable and pleasant. Despite my love of literature, of good writers, I've always appreciated good orators. There's something very graceful and skilled about connecting with the masses aloud, just like priests do. I realize my social inadequacies by merely being in her audience, and start feeling insecure about my life all over again. How did I end up a professor?

Jack is sitting near the front. I don't recognize the students on either side of him, so I'm certain he doesn't know them, either. Jack consults his paper program after the Dean concludes her opening remarks. "We'll now have the presentation of the student scholars. I invite each of the students to make brief remarks about their time at the University of Michigan and their plans for the future. I'm sure we'll all be listening with great interest," she says, her eyes twinkling.

I scan the program. Jack is scheduled to go second to last. Eleven others will go before him, and I will indeed listen with great interest. There are two planning phases in a young adult's life that often speak to their character: post-high school plans, and post-college plans, although neither period is as major as they think it is.

I sit and listen, often in a quiet wonder. One young lady is off to the Congo region to help Doctors Without Borders. One young man accepted a research appointment at Harvard to work on heart disease advancements. Another young man is opening up a free community center for disadvantaged youth in Detroit with money he raised at his part-time job. My wonder slips into nostalgia. Then hesitation. And finally, regret. I remember my grand post-college plans: more school, more borrowed time, and a commitment to join Brian wherever he wanted to lead me. I didn't have any noble prospects, and frankly, I still don't.

But I'm pitiful only temporarily. Soon I'm overwhelmed with anxiety and concern, wishing for a mug of spiked peppermint tea anywhere but here. What will Jack say? If I don't know his plans, does he know? He can't go up to the podium without saying something.

I start to fidget. I read the program over and over and over again, now wishing I stayed at home. I remember my purpose and turn on my camera. Jack's up next.

Applause throbs. I lift my head. Jack's muscular body walks up to the podium, his hands fingering an imaginary clarinet for the briefest of moments. He does this when he's nervous, and I've always loved that little piece of him. I am nervous, too.

The Dean announces his name. He accepts his certificate and adjusts the microphone.

"Thank you," he remarks sweetly. "I must admit I'm feeling rather lackluster after hearing about my fellow students' plans," he begins. Me too, Jack. "But I will say that my four years here were spent well. This school and Ann Arbor gave me a lot of inspiration."

I snap a quick photo. The red curtain behind him looks wonderful in the shot, such a brilliant backdrop. He's almost a celebrity right now, a hunk from a tabloid.

"Outside of the classroom, I spent much of my time rehearsing music in a beautiful old house by the river, and occupying orchestra chairs in Thursday and Saturday night concerts. I haven't told many people yet, but I've written a symphony. I plan to spend the next year finding an orchestra willing to play it."

My camera falls to my lap. "What?" I say aloud, too loudly, piercingly audible in the still auditorium, alive only with intent ears, a room full of university folk eager to hear about the birth of a new symphony.

Jack's eyes meet mine. He squints across the room of heads, his mouth ajar. I see him swallow with recognition. I see him look down. He does not look happy.

He looks up at me once more, cocking his head to the side. He clears his throat. "I also spent a lot of time chasing love," he continues, somber now, uncomfortably so. "Sometimes you just can't help chasing love, even if you know your object of affection couldn't care less." The room is tense, but softens with his emerging youthful smile. "Maybe I'll see about obtaining love, too," he says, but his eyes grow dark again as they find mine.

He raises his hand, his finger uncurling into a point. "My symphony is for her," Jack announces. A curious gasp firecrackers through the auditorium, and at once, two hundred sets of eyes are on me, on my skin, on my lips, and on my age, so much older than Jack. My colleagues look confused, intrigued, disgusted. I am ready to die. The room is so taken by me, an eagle could fly in and land without notice.

Jack reaches the finale of tonight's symphony. "It's for you, Mae. I hope you like it."

And once again, my life changes.

CHAPTER
6

When I started stealing Communion bread, I just kept a few wafers in my bedroom. Probably three or four wafers. I never ate them, or did anything with them. The wafers went stale, and got a little turned up at the edges; then they just sat there, taking up a little space but giving me a lot of comfort.

I reflect on this while organizing my new chest of drawers from Dale, which now houses, according to the legal ledger propped up next to me, a full two thousand and thirty-three Communion wafers. All of those little boxes I stored away in my bedroom dresser really added up; I only took a handful of wafers at a time from churches. They are now cataloged in little baggies by date, each baggie labeled and carefully folded to let out as much air as possible so that I can store even more wafers. But I still don't have a good locking system, just a steel rod and padlock that I found in the basement from an old fishing tackle box. I'm going to need to figure this out, to take the right precautions. I should probably go back to the hardware store and poke around.

After my wafer index is updated, I drag my new television into my bedroom. I'm definitely more energetic today. The Pope's funeral coverage is on, somewhat adjusted for time zone differences, though whether live or not the reporting is around the clock. Everyone is in Vatican City, ready for an interview, ready to watch the processional and the orchestrated mass. World leaders of all faiths and from all places fulfilling their expected requirement; dutiful pilgrims from all walks of life still hoping for salvation; and journalists from every station around the globe with stories and perspectives to share about the newly dead, excited to add this to their career timelines.

But I'm in Ann Arbor, my bedroom door locked, Oscar at my side. I'm trying to forget about the brazen spectacle that Jack put me through last night. I haven't seen him since he stood in front of that red curtain and betrayed me, professed his lust for me like an entitled twenty-two-year-old, disregarding the consequences of such a relationship. I refuse to call it "love" even if he thinks it's love, because Jack has never loved anyone; of this I'm sure. I ducked out when he finished his acceptance speech, nauseated and disgusted, still two hundred sets of eyes on me, the deviant older professor. I didn't hear the thirteenth student accept his award, and I'm pretty sure no one actually listened to him.

After class this morning, where I collected completed exams from outgoing seniors, I checked my faculty mailbox and certainly expected paperwork calling for my dismissal. I've already been rehearsing an articulate defense, stating that nothing ever happened between us, inviting those in charge to come over for a home visit to talk this through over pasta salad and lemon water. But my mailbox was empty, as was the faculty lounge I walked through to get to the mailbox. The department secretary smiled at me, and I sensed she was unaware of the unfolding circumstances. Well, it's hard to fire someone on a Friday; that's a lot of paperwork for a Friday. Maybe my demise will come on Monday, after the graduation ceremony is in the past.

Also, I'm unaware of Jack's whereabouts, and couldn't be happier that he's missing.

Another Pope montage begins on the screen, this time depicting John Paul II's early years. His kindness, so permanent, so innate, is evident in every shot. There's even a photo of him graduating from seminary.

A symphony. When? I listen to Jack rehearse. I watch Jack study. I attend his concerts. I cook his dinners. When was something so big happening? How long is this symphony? Is it in a major key? Is it in a minor key? If it's for me, then is it also *about* me? There are so many difficult conversations ahead, while that little shit is running around town.

Soon I'm up and moving, determined to settle this matter. I think I've got about an hour until they're actually putting the Pope into his tomb, until the live theater ends, though this probably won't be shown. I creak back down the hallway, as I have for years, and stop in front of Jack's room. Today the bed is made, the papers are in a tidy pile, the clarinet is still. It feels like trespassing to enter Jack's room, just like breaking into St. Paul's, though I feel less guilty breaking into churches than snooping in his bedroom.

I start by pawing through his plastic bin of loose sheet music. Everything here is already published. Names of well-known and little-known composers are stamped at the top, and Jack has written all over each piece, adding his own embellishments, crossing out notes and writing in new notes, creating musical phrases. No original symphony here. And I'm sure some of these composers would have fits about the liberties Jack has taken.

I work on his desk next, though it's mostly full of old assignments and books. There's a stack of library books in the back. Curious, I sift through the titles: *Moby Dick, The British Encyclopedia of Composers, Anne of Green Gables* (really?), and finally, *Diagnosing Mental Disorders*.

I cock my head at this last book, wondering why he'd take out such material. He had a general psychology class freshman year, but not anything related since. Is he feeling a little too self-reflective? Is his mind on the list of women he burns through each year, some for sex, others to control? As I run my finger down the spine, I see he's stuck a yellow scrap of paper in the middle to mark a section. Swiftly, I open to this placeholder.

The chapter title reads: "Diagnosing Schizophrenia." I scan the introduction. The author notes that schizophrenia patients have altered perceptions of reality. They have hallucinations, or delusions. They see things that aren't there, hear voices that aren't speaking. I nod in agreement, remembering my own freshman year psychology class. As I turn the page, engrossed in the "Causes of Schizophrenia" section, I see the author has provided a diagnostic quiz to help discern if someone might have the disorder, or perhaps a closely related disorder instead.

There are light pencil markings over many of the ovals. Someone has checked off most of the symptoms, including "psychotic episodes where the patient's mind is in another place altogether, completely removed from the actual here and now." Next to this symptom, a scribble reveals: "Claimed corn was pelting the car. Almost killed us on the road."

The book makes a sharp thump as it hits the floor, the pages bending like fanned bridges. I raise my hand to my face, feeling my cheekbones, rubbing up to my temples. Jack has taken this quiz on my behalf.

I stare at the book's cover. There's a serious-looking doctor holding a clipboard. A chalkboard stands behind him, full of carefully chosen medical terminology. It's silly looking. It's definitely just stock photography. Is Jack going to try to admit me somewhere? Does Jack think I'm dangerous?

I realize now that it's a good thing Jack is leaving soon. We have to go our separate ways. He affects me, and I affect him, permanently.

*

John Paul II lies still and pale, his head on three pillows, his coffin tipped so more eyes can see him one last time. What a strange job, what an eerie life, preparing a coffin for the dead, preparing the dead for the ground. The announcers tell us that soon he'll be taken away by the pallbearers. "It's almost time," they keep saying, informing us that we've reached the end. I sigh and say my goodbye, not wanting that last final glimpse of his body to stay with me.

The front door slams just as I turn off the television. I hear the familiar sound of Jack throwing his keys on my walnut end table, scratched from the abuse its taken over the years. The table top knows the metallic graze of keys and glasses, has soaked up spilled wine and coffee, persevered through Oscar's sinking nails. Jack even kicked the table once, when a girl, standing so delicately in my doorframe, told him he was a "fucking asshole" before she left the house.

Jack is noisy. He stomps to the answering machine, checking for messages that never arrive. He stomps further, over and into his room, where the psychology book is now carefully replaced at the bottom of the library stack. I'm always careful to cover my tracks.

I hear Jack coming my way, slowly, heavily. Jack is at my door now, waiting.

I watch the doorknob turn, like the earth rotating on its axis. I'm in no mood for this, and should have locked it again. My Pope is dead, and my tenant is awful.

Jack comes to me, looking strange, looking sick. Now he has a cross to bear.

"Wanted to give you a copy of this," he says, handing me a photograph of the two of us at that rusty campground outside of town.

I place it on my nightstand.

"I'm sorry, Mae," he says. "I should have told you about the symphony."

I look at Jack, really look at him. For all his intelligence, for all his accomplishments, his mind is still young, his heart younger still.

"Jack, are you serious? This is not about the symphony. I could lose my job after the way you suggested we're together. I'd have to leave, start over, and who would hire me with such a dirty background? Why are you incapable of understanding other people? Why are you so reckless?"

Jack is still, expressionless.

"What will it take," I say, so very coldly, as plainly as possible, "for you to stop hurting people? For you to put someone else first?"

Jack's eyes fall downward. Everything is so poignantly silent now, and for the first time, I'm able to imagine life without him. It'll be quiet. I'll have my routine. I won't take another tenant; I can't chance this again.

"Mae," Jack says, "do you know that I have feelings for you? That I really do love you?"

I answer quickly. "I've picked up that you're into me, yes." We've lived together well over three years, and now, finally, we're having the conversation we should have had at the start. Jack's always shown an interest in me. But I'm to blame for letting it carry on so long.

Jack's face shifts to anger, alive with fuel and strength. "Mae, I am in love with you. In. Love. With. You. Please, this is so difficult for me—"

"Jack, you can't possibly be in love with me. If you actually loved me, you wouldn't—"

"Mae. Goddamn it. What is so hard to believe about a guy loving a beautiful, older, off-limits woman? You teach English literature. Surely you've read this story before. It happens."

I wasn't expecting this. For a moment, several moments, I'm speechless and lost in revolving thoughts.

"I take your silence to mean you don't have feelings for me, Mae."

I look at Jack, standing so earnestly now. "No, Jack," I say directly, "I don't have feelings for you. I care about your well-being and your life, but I am not attracted to you. I don't want you. And I'm eager to live alone again."

Jack disappears into the hallway and down the stairs.

*

I ate by myself tonight. Jack ate on the pier, examining planks between bites, a hammer in his back pocket. As the sun tucks itself away, exhausted after another day of illuminating the world for sightless people like us, I tuck Jack's gun into my jeans and stride down the driveway. The house looks worried behind me.

I noticed Jack had a gun last year, when we were walking through the woods to collect firewood for the winter. I saw it sticking out of his belt. I wasn't afraid; strangely, I wasn't even terribly interested. I merely said, "Does that gun stay in my house?" He nodded. That was it. I won't argue with a gun in my house when I feel so oddly watched and uneasy.

"I keep it in my desk drawer, just in case I need it," Jack went on. I didn't ask for further clarification. I remembered its whereabouts, and tonight, I slid it out of the hickory drawer as easily as grabbing a postage stamp.

I have unfinished business at St. Paul's. The walk is focused tonight, empty tonight. Usually I pass a few neighbors tugging at weeds or rolling their wheelbarrows in for the day. Tonight, I have a fragmented moon for company, and a soft wind at my back. I have walked this sidewalk for years: hopeful about the world, dismal about the world, obsessed with changing the world, valiantly forgetting the world. Some walks were at the peak of my life, while others, like tonight, feel low, but necessary.

The churchyard is just ahead. A few summers ago I traveled to Ireland and was captivated by the many abbeys sprinkled throughout the countryside: some in decent shape, others in ruin, but nobody would dare tear down a holy, historic place, and so they stand, waiting to see who might pay them attention before they crumble completely. Most are surrounded by graveyards, elaborate Celtic crosses marking resting places. These too are often crumbling, but the occasional fresh flower bouquet tells us there are visitors, there are descendants. It is particularly eerie when an abbey stands in a field of hay or barley, cows wandering around the property as if it is an extension of their barn. I view Ann Arbor in the same manner: what will remain four hundred years from now? Will my house make it? Will St. Paul's still stand here?

I walk up the paved path to the side door. Like a banker working a safe, my hands punch in the code. The light remains red, the door remains still. I try a few former codes, as I know the priest rotates through them. Again, the light remains red. I pull Jack's gun from my pocket, aim the barrel at the door lock, and pull the trigger. With a terrific pop, a steaming hole is left, warm air from the church now pushing out to mingle with the cooler air outside. The door opens easily.

I have never fired a gun before. It isn't as difficult as I imagined.

Inside the foyer, I crouch down to pick up the metal fragments and a warped bullet melted around a chunk from the lock, but drop the pile quickly. They're too hot, too sharp. I take off my sweatshirt, similar to the one I used to wrap my fist before considering whether or not to smash a window out of this church a few days ago. Guns are much more efficient, but the sweatshirt is useful for picking up evidence. After I've collected the pieces, I open my floral handbag and dump the bits right in.

As I walk deeper into the church, it finally occurs to me to look behind my shoulder, to see if anyone is around. I'm getting clumsier, duller on the inside. I can see the churchyard and it looks empty. The broken door is my only concern now, and I wonder if I've left any prints behind. I consider going back to investigate when I hear footsteps coming up the far back steps, close to the altar. I jog into the adjacent dark nursery, waiting with fright.

I'm in a terrible place now. I can hear the priest sobbing, and the broken door is swinging open and closed, open and closed as he leaves and enters. I hear him praying in Latin. Jack knows a bit of Latin. I do, too, and make out the words for "Lord," "soul," and "mercy." It's so dark in the nursery that I can't see anything at all now. It's windowless, and I am without an outline. If it weren't for my breathing, toxic and jagged, I'd be perfectly invisible. It's terrifying in this room. The cops will probably come soon, and I'll be stuck here, in the sticky darkness, just waiting.

Minutes pass. I think about going home. I wonder if I'll ever be the same again. The foyer is now quiet beyond the nursery. After the slowest, most careful, most quiet walk of my life, I get on my knees and peek under the doorframe. It's dim. I hear nothing, see nothing, though my view is very limited. I have to leave or I'll be stuck indefinitely. With a swallow and sinner's hands, I push open the door and stretch my face out an inch, still protected in shadows.

The foyer is empty, the church is on pause. The altar is alone, and the Apostles hanging around the room are alone, too, their eyes now shut, their minds plastic and abandoned. They are not lively like they once were, the last time I trespassed in St. Paul's.

The priest is gone, the cops aren't here, or perhaps haven't even been summoned, though that bang out front was certainly loud enough. With one last look at the damage from the gun, I move into the sanctuary.

I'm keenly aware that time is short, that my safety net is small and growing smaller. I get to the front, passing all those first-name guys as I go: Pete, Andy, Jim. They refuse to look at me tonight, refuse to guide me. No matter; I can get by on my own.

I walk up the altar steps and stop at the back wall of the church. I've never noticed the wallpaper before, but there are tiny crosses embellishing the tan stripes. These crosses are much smaller than the one I'm about to deal with.

Under the raised roof soaring into the heavens, I inhale and look up, staring at the five-foot wooden cross nailed down in front of me.

"It has to be done," I reassure myself, taking a hammer out of my handbag before violently prying the giant cross off the wall, nails landing at my feet.

*

Four police cars idle on Mae Harrington's front lawn, deep tire ruts in the grass jutting out behind them. Red and blue lights bounce off Mae's windows and onto her neighbors' houses. Jack is standing on the stoop, hands in his pockets, eyes pained. Father Duling is talking to the police in his street clothes, obviously quite upset.

"I'm certain it was her," he tells an officer. "She's been up to no good in my church for years." The officer takes notes while Jack listens, wondering when he'll see Mae again, feeling he may never see Mae again. Jack swallows and backs into the doorframe, walking through the sullen house alone. The shadows are long tonight, the air unsettled. He enters his bedroom, stepping over yellow police tape. As soon as the call from the station came, Jack knew his gun would be gone. He walks to his desk, now a piece of evidence already wiped for fingerprints, and grabs his address book from the top. He flips through it as he walks to the kitchen phone.

Jack's fingers dial the unfamiliar numbers. She answers after one ring.

"Hi, Mom," Jack says, his voice sounding young. "I'm really sorry, but you can't stay here tomorrow night."

*

The cross is awkward. I've got it slung over one shoulder, but it's oddly bottom-heavy; turns out the big Jesus on top is made from some kind of light crafting styrofoam, so the weighty bottom keeps slipping down to the sidewalk with a horrible thump. I have no idea how this stayed up on the church's wall. I'm sure the wood is chipping now. I'm sure my back will pulse from this in the morning. I feel like a character in a play, dragging the cross for comedy. I'm happy the streets are vacant, house lights mostly off. Perhaps everyone is at campus attending early graduation events.

I hobble along, the cross occasionally swatting some bushes or droopy tulips lining the sidewalk. The path is uneven here, making my work more difficult. A few blocks from home, I'm able to make the turn into Nora Park, deserted and waiting for me.

I can see the pond, the pond where the girl drowned, the gargoyle said. Ducks float on the black water, paired up for the mating season. I hear a few bugs, and some leftover leaves blowing across the grass that never got raked up last fall before snow covered the park. I imagine a few families came by earlier to play softball or frisbee in the sunny afternoon.

Relief is close. I've felt so guilty these past few weeks, intensely so, worse than the last few decades combined. The cross bruised my shoulder blade, but it's almost home. It's far too dark to see into the water, but I'm confident I'll place it correctly for her and she won't be lonely anymore.

I stop at the edge, finally able to lower the cross and stand beside it. It's quite thick and sturdy, and I'm surprised I managed to carry it all those blocks alone. I pivot the base, lining it up to fall perfectly. "I hope He helps you," I whisper, releasing the cross with satisfaction. It lands with a tremendous splash, and I'm glad that it sinks, disappearing out of view.

Air bubbles float to the surface and I'm content to watch for a while, imagining the wood settling into the muddy bottom. The ducks left the water some time ago, now watching me suspiciously from beneath the willow trees. I don't see any styrofoam bits from Jesus rise to the top of the water, so I'm free to leave.

I walk swiftly toward my house, which is just around the bend now. As my property comes into view, I stop, instantly stunned. Cop cars are lined up on my grass. Several neighbors are standing in their bathrobes, arms gesturing. I've caused a crime scene. I am a crime scene.

In a panic I walk backward, quietly stepping into the cover of trees. I'm about to run when I hear him.

"Hello Mae," he says, his voice so distinct, each syllable slightly separated. I turn around, so nervous now that I feel like I'm having an out-of-body experience. The paperboy is grinning at me, his eyes fixated on my face. He licks his lips. His tail, lean and scaled, is making figure eights on the cement. "So you went down to the park, did you?" he asks.

"I did," I tell him, studying his body. "It was too dark to look for her, but I sent her company."

The paperboy is still grinning, his monster-body surreal in the shade of night. "That was very thoughtful of you, Mae."

I'm still able to see the events in my yard. I have to get out of here.

"It was worth it, Mae," the paperboy continues. "Don't worry about the police. And certainly don't worry about Jack."

I turn to face him, doing all I can to force myself into awareness, into the here and now. "I know you're not real," I finally say.

The paperboy looks hurt, and mopey. "Oh, I'm quite real, Mae," he says, giving his tail a good flick. "I'm just not human."

I've lost. Lonesome, regretful, I give my house one last look, its white exterior flashing blue and red, blue and red. More than anything else, I've loved living here, loved caring for something, and will miss the normalcy of all that severely.

"I have to go now," I tell the paperboy.

"I understand," he says. "And you do know, that you shouldn't come back. Ever."

Our eyes meet again: mine stinging, his clear. I let go of this moment and walk past the demon on the sidewalk, moving on into the Ann Arbor indigo.

CHAPTER 7

I walk through the night, stopping only to take out my $500 daily limit from an ATM on the edge of town. Thankfully I had quite a bit in my wallet already.

Currently, I'm walking west. My mind is on Chicago. The last time I was in Chicago, I felt the magic, intellectualness, and joy one can only feel in the Midwest's largest city. It was a long weekend away from campus, and Brian was at my side. Visiting the popular museums, enjoying the view from the top of the Sears Tower, reveling in local beer, sampling the town's best pizza; it was all very satisfying. We didn't feel rushed, or stressed like I do when I visit New York. A few locals even offered to take our picture in front of landmarks after we tried to ourselves, arms outstretched, giggles flowing because my head was never in the frame. I'm pretty sure that Brian is living in Chicago now. I just see him there, feel his creative talents bubbling up from that place. He seemed so comfortable in Chicago, and so happy that I gave him a break from the competition of star-lusting Los Angeles. "You can sing anywhere," I told him. "The human voice is very portable."

As the sun starts peeking over the horizon, creating a soft glow over the treetops and fading stars, I stop at a little diner that is just opening its window shades for the day. A few semis are already lined up, drivers ready to scoop up eggs and pinch bacon between their fingers. I'm not certain which town I'm in, but it's definitely time to sit down now.

I take a seat by the window. My legs started hurting hours ago, but now they've melted into a sort of nice numbness, like invisible ice packs are taped to my knees. My big toe on my right foot is bleeding, but I feel capable all the same.

A waitress stops to get me started on a big mug of coffee, its aroma instantly enticing. "Morning," she says, her smile genuine but her fatigue apparent. "Want a menu?"

I nod and inspect my laminated sheet. I thought about many things on my walk, but most often, I focused on my current situation. Specifically, have I simply run away, or am I actually wanted by the police? Breaking and entering is no small crime, and stealing the cross was rather bold, but I'm sure the physical damages are only $1,000 or so. Will someone come looking for me, or will I just have a police record that will stay with me like my other problems? Will the police show up here while I'm eating my breakfast, hauling me out in handcuffs with syrup on my chin, or will I just have a problem getting a loan later? Maybe I'll just receive a bill in the mail, with a perforated invoice slip to mail back.

Of course, I'm thinking about Jack, too. As much as he troubles me, angers me, causes me conflict that I can't resolve, I do feel guilty about the predicament I've put him in. Now he'll have to stay and look after my place. He'll feel obligated to.

And it's graduation weekend.

His mother probably isn't coming over for graduation anymore, considering the mess I've left behind. I do hope he goes to his graduation ceremony. What a shame. How selfish of me. I was going to make that woman's bed, too. I was even going make a fancy roast for the table, served on my nice formal platter with handles. Glazed carrots, sprigs of rosemary, all of that.

I watch the waitress, who is still assembling silverware packets for the day. She wipes off water stains on her apron, carefully tucking each spoon, knife, and fork into its little triangle house. After a few triangles, and a few smiles to incoming customers who I presume are regulars, she returns to me.

"What'll it be?" she wants to know.

"I'll take a western omelette and short stack," I say, sliding my menu toward her.

She writes down my order before saying, "I haven't seen you before. Everyone that comes in at this time is either an old friend or a trucker getting started on their day. You got a rig parked outside?"

I imagine myself trying to maneuver a semi when I have trouble driving my own car. Couldn't take it over any bridges, that's for sure. "No," I say, "I came here on foot."

The waitress looks at me strangely, and I realize it's an odd hour for a walk. She chuckles before saying, "Yeah, you look too expensive for the trucker life." She refills my coffee and takes my order to the waiting cook.

Strange that I look expensive with these sweaty and wrinkled pants, messy from a night of clipping along on the shoulder of the road. But as I scope out the place, it's apparent that I'm at least overdressed, hamper pants and all. Some of the men in this diner are absolutely filthy, completely soiled from head to toe as they sit solo in their booths and on their stools. They wear scrappy flannel, and faded stripes, and plainly stained t-shirts, sipping black coffee between thick beards and mustaches, waiting for their griddle specials and thinking about the road. How does a trucker get so filthy? Are they doing farm work on the side?

My window affords me a view of the parking lot, an asphalt and gravel combination with weeds growing among the cracks and potholes. The marquee shows a rib eye dinner special tonight for $8.99. Much like I wouldn't order lobster in the Midwest that costs under $20, I wouldn't order a steak for less than $20, either. I'm also particularly weary of roving food trucks that sell boxed lunches to office workers, Mexican restaurants with carne asada strips on revolving racks under heat lamps, and most shrimp cocktail offerings.

But back in Los Angeles, right in the thick of my literature and food education, I loved those roving food trucks. I loved the hunt of trying to find my favorite carnita truck, driving slowly up and down the trucker's neighborhood until I found him and those little sizzling rolls stuffed with pork and dripping with green salsa. There was also a very popular club in Los Angles that offered a martini glass full of shrimp and sauce for $1.99. My friends and I thought this was the greatest public service the city offered. Brian always ordered two. The differences between then and now hit me as I sink down into the booth, which already feels so sticky, like a flypaper trap for humans.

I often think about the friends I used to have back then, the select few who were always up for an ambling adventure, a heated political discussion, or a morning at the beach just taking up space on the sand. As I grew closer to Brian and longed for a more settled life, I chose isolation with Brian over friends, even eventually leaving beautiful Nora behind. Now, I'm choosing further isolation. Nothing seems out of the ordinary here in this trucker's haven, nothing seems disturbed here. Perhaps being out of my house and away from Ann Arbor really will do me some good, and being alone will finally feel just right.

My omelette arrives, and it's quite tasty—eggs from greasy spoon diners usually are. I decide I'll keep walking, southwest, in hopes of reaching Chicago by the end of next week. Although, it'd be much faster to hitch a ride with one of these truckers, who are now occupying all the seats. Surely one of them is off to a hub like Chicago, ready to drop off a load of pipes or pick up old city parts. Inquiring without sounding like a prostitute looking for a trade could be difficult, though. As I look from face to face, searching for a gentle one, a harmless one, the waitress turns on the diner's old Sylvania television set.

After a few commercials the local morning news fills the screen. The truckers lift their heads in unison.

"And in from Ann Arbor, police are looking for an armed suspect. A University of Michigan professor is on the run after breaking into a local church. Details are still forthcoming about the exact nature of her crime, but she is considered a threat."

Drowning shock washes over me. I look at the ceiling, expecting a spotlight to illuminate my body, to tell the world my whereabouts.

My eyes return to the television screen, sick and guilty. An older staff photo of me pops into the lower corner, one suitable for studying or distributing on posters. A policeman is standing on the sidewalk outside my house, his pale skin shiny in the morning light. Did the cops stay there all night? I scan the background, hoping to see Jack. The policeman speaks.

"Based on her history of mental illness, we are alerting the public that she is armed and should be considered dangerous. If you see her, please call 911 immediately. This is a preventative measure in hopes that her situation won't escalate."

I would never kill anyone! Is that what he's implying—that I could be pushed to kill? I feel the gun through my handbag, making sure it's still accounted for. My shock is swirling into anger now. I shake my head frantically and look at the bill, quite ready to leave. Seeing me fish in my wallet, the dutiful waitress returns. I hope with all of my overflowing energy that she doesn't recognize me in that old photo.

"Crazy about the Michigan professor, huh?" she says, waiting for my cash.

"She's not crazy," I say, handing over my money.

"Guess we'll see after they say what she's done," the waitress replies, stepping out of my way. "Thanks, dear. You have a good day and come back any time for another omelette."

I head outside and look for the nearest motel.

*

Back in Ann Arbor, the news crews are dispersing. Jack is sitting at Mae's kitchen table, stirring an Earl Gray tea while yet another investigator questions him. The police stayed at Mae's house all night, everyone now bleary-eyed and tense from a lack of sleep.

The investigator turns on his recorder and opens his notepad. "Jack, thanks again for your cooperation. I just have a few more questions and then we'll leave you alone unless circumstances change."

Jack nods, wondering if he'll get to bed anytime soon, wondering if he'll ever sleep properly again.

"Jack, do you think Mae is a religious fanatic?"

These strong words sting Jack, these labels and assumptions about Mae. All the same, it's an expected question.

"I do think so, yes," Jack answers.

"And do you think she is capable of murdering someone?"

The pain is surreal, hearing such language about someone as precious as Mae. Jack reflects on the past three years, on Mae as a professor and Mae as a friend. He thinks about her angry times, her relentless times, and finally answers, "No, I don't think she is capable of murder, nor would that ever be her agenda."

Jack can see the pier from the table, still waiting for his help. Perhaps tomorrow. Perhaps if he carries on their plans and his daily routine, she'll come home as she always does, tossing her keys on the walnut end table.

The investigator asks another question that stuns Jack into grief. "Do you think Mae is capable of destroying a church, perhaps using an explosive, like a domestic terrorist?"

Mae the terrorist.

Jack scratches his face, sore from fatigue and confusion. Oscar strolls in and over to his empty food dish, wondering when breakfast is coming. It's been so nice for Jack to have company for breakfast on the weekends, sitting at this table, looking down over the water.

Jack answers, "I really don't know if she'd blow anything up. But she has some serious problems with religion."

"It seems that way," the investigator remarks. "Does she ever talk about Heaven or Hell? Like, if she'll go to either one, or who she thinks belongs there?"

Jack tips his head, thinking this over. "I think she believes in both, because she seems keen that there is always a balance, always good and evil. I wouldn't be surprised if she thinks Heaven is right up there in the clouds, though, just a nice plane ride away."

"With angels playing harps?" the investigator wants to know.

"Probably not harps," Jack says.

*

I awake in the late afternoon, asleep under a worn floral bedspread at a ten-room motel. I'm in unit eight, toward the back. I believe I'm the only guest. This is exactly the kind of motel that criminals gravitate toward—the sleepy, forgotten kind where they can lie low.

Before succumbing to sleep, I washed out my clothes using the motel's generic free shampoo. My clothes are drying over the shower rod now, dripping onto the tiled floor. The motel is old, and small, but it's clean and has a nice view of the woods. I walk over to the window, running my fingernails over the metal screen. I notice little push-tabs on the sides; these screens would pop off easily, should it come to that. Why do I take Christ as such a literal figure? Why do I need bread and crosses to believe? My faith is absent, my situation dire.

I didn't need any identification to check-in at this motel, something that worried me a great deal as I entered the lobby, though the chances of many seeing the early morning news is slim. Of course, I may appear in the paper tomorrow. Surely I will, as this is decent news for the area, and has the makings for great gossip: a female professor goes nuts, and is now on the lam with a gun. What perfect fodder for any conversation, especially when the media picks up on my young male tenant.

I turn on the room's television. I lived without a television for ten years, and now it's my main interest and security line. I search for a phone book, wondering if there's another restaurant in the area. I could return to the diner, just a mile away, but I'd be faced with the rib eye special and possibly recognition. I decide ordering cheap pizza and a bottle of soda is fine for the evening, though I'll have to wait until my clothes are dry before I answer the door.

The local evening news interests me a great deal, the same channel that told my story and circumstances this morning. The volume is up and I'm focused on each word, sore from my journey so far and slouched on the end of the bed. There's a story about an elementary school kid, and the annual animal shelter charity drive, and highlights of national and world news, but I'm never mentioned. I feel relief, but also worry that this silence is only temporary. I wonder if the police have gone through all my things, have touched all my possessions and pieced together my life through Jack's recounting. I wonder if my bread is safe, and I'm wondering how Jack is spending his last hours as a student.

Soon I order my pizza and break my rules to read the only material available: *The Holy Bible.*

CHAPTER 8

At the Central Police Station in downtown Detroit, Captain Douglas reviews the notes from the professor case in Ann Arbor. That's what everyone is calling it around here: "The Professor Case." And although there's no crafty murder involved or a searing tale of unforgivable-ness, there's something really compelling about a respected woman going off the deep end. It's not every day you hear about a woman dragging a giant cross out of a church that she just blew open with a gun. Sure beats processing endless drug citations and reading about the next round of budget cuts.

Douglas has a sharp mind and a baby tooth for an incisor. He reads the timeline of events and interview answers from neighbors, Father Duling, and Jack. This isn't his jurisdiction, but he told the detectives he'd do what he could to help. He got his start as an Ann Arbor officer and is quite familiar with Mae's quaint neighborhood.

He picks up his phone, dialing the head investigator's number. "Captain Douglas, from Detroit. Say, let's keep the media in the dark from now on about the professor. If she's become interested in television, she's surely seen herself on the news by now. If she thinks we've forgotten about her, she'll be more likely to visit another church."

The investigator agrees. "Will do, bro."

"Any new leads about her whereabouts?"

"Maybe. We think she'll head to Chicago at some point. The only photos she keeps around the house are of the Windy City, space, and some little campground she visited with Jack. There isn't a single photo of an unknown person around, so she probably won't head to a friend's house to hide."

The Captain laughs. "Space, huh? Well, she'll have to deal with a whole new set of laws if she leaves the planet. Hey, when are you interviewing her colleagues?"

The investigator sighs. "They're a little hard to get ahold of right now, seeing as it's Graduation Sunday on Michigan's campus. Hopefully tomorrow."

*

It's a new day, and I'm standing in the motel's lobby, freshly showered and full of cold pizza. There's a nice map of the Midwest on the wall, with routes to destination points clearly labeled in a manner I'm grateful for in my time of disorder. The front clerk steps up to the desk.

"Morning. All set to leave?"

I nod. "Yes. Do you know where the nearest Amtrak or Greyhound station is?"

The clerk rings up my bill. "There's a big hub over in Ann Arbor," she says. I silently scowl.

"Anything this direction or to the south?"

The clerk thinks for a moment. "You know, I think there's a Greyhound depot in Jackson."

"How far is that?"

"Oh, about a thirty-minute drive."

Now I think for a moment. "Probably too far to walk?"

The clerk nods strongly. "Yes, too far to walk."

I take my receipt and step outside, ready for my long walk. I-94 would be quickest, but I can't walk along the highway. I start heading west, enjoying the clear, slightly cool day that I know will explode with humidity before noon. My head was swirling with concerns during and after dinner last night, but I fell asleep as soon as I crawled back under that worn floral bedspread. Vigorous walking can be a wonderful sedative, feeling tender muscles growing heavier and duller.

But seeing as my legs absolutely ache from yesterday, I'd rather not walk the distance ahead of me, and certainly not vigorously. I should have called a cab. I do love exploring little gas station towns, though—the kind of towns where a gas station and a few houses dotting the countryside are all there is to see at first glance. I find these kinds of towns often have fascinating casts of characters, the kinds of people who've never left the county, much less the country, and are scared of "the thugs in mean Detroit." I got a flat tire in an area like this once, and found myself having lemonade with a man who was convinced the local area high school was really a military holding tank for prisoners of war. I'm sure many of the school's students would agree with him. Then again, I'm starting to realize I'm no judge of character or class anymore, seeing as I'm taking advice from a gargoyle demon.

Fraying dandelions are struggling to survive on this country road, my sneakers kicking their seeds into the wind for a second chance. I'm actually walking at a nice pace, all things considered, helped by the early morning temperate weather and fantasies about more home-cookin' diner food. Soon a car slows to a stop beside me.

"Ma'am, you need a ride somewhere, or are you out exercising?"

His comment makes me smile. Once when I was legitimately exercising around my neighborhood, another Michigander asked if I needed a ride somewhere, too. Apparently my water bottle and headphones weren't enough to tip him off.

The man seems friendly enough in his ball cap and U of M sweatshirt. His pickup truck is clean and his oral health is good. "Well, I need to get to Jackson. I had . . . car trouble."

That sounds too general and unconvincing, but the man is motioning me over anyway. "Have to go to Jackson sooner or later to pick up chicken feed. Might as well be today."

I climb in beside him, hoping he won't be much of a talker. Seems I won't luck out this morning; he's one of those who wants to ask me everything and tell me even more. "So, where you from? Whatcha do for a living?"

How to answer? While under the worn floral bedspread, I told myself that if lying must occur, it must be consistent and boring. Don't paint an extravagant life for yourself. Don't be memorable. Don't be worth talking to for long.

"I'm a bank teller in Lansing. Just over here visiting a friend."

The man nods. "I'm Bruce," he says, reaching his hand sideways to shake mine.

"Maggie," I say, quickly regretting the name I chose. I hope he doesn't start humming Rod Stewart's *Maggie May*.

Bruce shifts in his seat. "Heard you folks in Lansing are having a bunch of trouble lately with your water. That right?"

I should have kept walking. Be general.

"Yeah, you heard right."

"Seems ridiculous the city can't give you clean drinking water. When babies are dying from lead, that's criminal. Hope you're not eating fish from local waters, Maggie."

I was not aware Lansing was in such a situation.

"Got any babies, Maggie? I got three myself."

Our conversation continues as we coast down I-94. I watch for passing gas station towns to mull over, and Bruce keeps pressing me for more life details. Temporary friendships are normally a joy. I love sitting next to someone new on an airplane, learning about their background, where they're heading, where they've been, and then happily wishing them well as we part ways in the noisy terminal. It's a minimal commitment, and a wonderful way to pass the time. Bruce is being a difficult temporary friend, however, in that he's dominating our conversation and not letting his temporary friend sit in silence and reflect for a spell; a necessary need under such close quarters.

Finally we pass a green highway sign that declares Jackson is just three miles away. Bruce asks, "Where should I drop you off?"

I'm about to say the Greyhound station, but that would be careless, and besides, I don't actually know where the Greyhound station is. I don't know where anything in Jackson is. My lips grow cracked under the stress. Then, a moment of clarity.

"I'll need a cup of coffee if I'm going to make it through this kind of day!" I say dramatically.

Bruce laughs and says, "I know just the place to drop you off then. It's a little burst of sunshine."

A few minutes later, I've thanked Bruce and am walking up the front path to *Betty's Coffee Shop*. What a charmer: a small house with a clean yellow exterior, white shutters, and potted plants on a button-cute porch. I pull the brass door handle and enter in a hopeful mood.

Inside I'm drawn to the lace curtains, the crisp linen tablecloths, the freshly cut flowers, and the wall paintings of orange fields. After confidently deciding that this place is a certified treasure, I read the perfect blackboard for today's specials.

The kitchen door opens mechanically, steadily widening on its own. In a moment, a woman in a wheelchair with snug brown hair glides through, turning gingerly into the dining room. She meets my eyes with a large smile.

"Hello there!" she says, coming closer. She has beautiful green eyes and a wonderful sense of joy about her. She is young. Perhaps thirty, but possibly younger. "I'm Betty! Ordering breakfast?"

We are alone. It's just past ten, that quiet time when most have eaten breakfast but it's too early for lunch. I hear a dishwasher humming in the distance. Betty is waiting for my answer.

I'm hungry, but don't want to bother her, don't want to make her keep wheeling around on my account. I'm guessing she'd absolutely hate my line of thinking. She'd be out of business if everyone felt this way about the disabled.

"Well, I'm mostly thirsty."

"Coffee then?"

"How about a bagel and coffee?" A gentle compromise.

"Very well," says Betty, backing up to head toward the cooler in the corner. I watch her remove a grabbing stick off the wall, then push the stick deep into the ice to fish out a small tub of cream cheese. She sets it on the counter before going back in for a wrapped bagel.

"Toasted, ma'am?" she calls over her shoulder.

"That'd be great," I say, feeling both awe and guilt.

As Betty works, I skim a newspaper another customer left behind. There's no mention of me. There is, however, a large picture of the University of Michigan's iconic Diag with the generic headline: "Graduates look to their future." I scan the accompanying photos of yesterday's smaller ceremonies, but recognize no one. I want all of the newspapers from the state, and all of the televisions I can get, each set to a different news station.

Betty returns, carefully unloading my items from a custom tray. "There you are," she says. "Let me know if you need anything else." And with that, she rolls her wheelchair back in the kitchen, and I am alone.

I've always been drawn to the disabled, strangely infatuated with their day-to-day lives. There was a man, in a church I used to go to, who was paralyzed from the waist down. His arm motion was limited, too. He'd always use his good hand to hold up his worse hand, his worse being his right, so he could properly shake hello. I learned he became paralyzed later in life, around fifty. He had to adjust, make do, start over. What struck me about him was his relentless energy and happy aura. He was always the first to church, and the last to go. He served as a greeter, a choir member, a coffee server, a tithings collector. He just took his time, and never lost his smile. He had a regular spot, by the far stained glass window, and on sunny mornings he positively glowed in warm yellow light. He laughed during funny parts of sermons, grew solemn during serious parts. He was, and remains, the most satisfied individual I have ever encountered. I think of him often. But I don't worry for him, as he has the kind of inner strength one sees so rarely in life. I could never be like him, or Betty, with her own restaurant despite her circumstances.

Betty returns to check up on me. I pay for my order and ask for directions to the Greyhound station. "You're in luck," she says. "It's only three blocks away."

During the three blocks, Betty's sweet and tidy life now in my past, I process the scenarios. Will someone check my ID? Will they *scan* my ID? Will a police blockade appear around the Indiana border, officers coming aboard to take me away while other passengers freak out and snap photos?

But my worries don't materialize. I pay with cash. I'm not asked for my ID. I have no bags, but those who do don't face baggage inspection—the duffels and suitcases are just loaded right under the bus. As I take my window seat, I wonder about our state's security, as there's a wanted criminal on board with a gun.

*

Finally alone in Ann Arbor, Jack locks all the doors and crawls into bed. But not his bed, since having to cross back and forth past fallen police tape is too stressful. Instead, Jack sleeps away the better part of the morning in Mae's bedroom, where some of her furniture was removed but the bed seems untouched and her door wasn't blocked. The pillows still smell like Mae.

He wakes just after noon. Exhausted, bewildered, and feeling sick, he barely stands upright. His graduation robe is hanging in the front closet. He decided before falling asleep that this day was still important, even if she's taken away his happiness. It's still worth walking across the stage. It's still worth it to find closure after this dramatic end.

He runs his hands over her new chest of drawers as he passes by, a piece that really doesn't match or go with anything in the house and was a curious buy. He snugs up the house—lights off, all doors locked—and leaves all this behind for a few hours.

Jack heads to the ceremony with purpose. North Campus is active and loud, with families gathering for photos, and friends in maize and blue huddled in celebration. Laughter, laughter. The Music School's satellite ceremony is close by, and Jack feels immediate anxiety upon seeing familiar faces. He's not sure who knows what. He doesn't know if the police have specifically alerted all the faculty about Mae. He doesn't feel like he belongs here right now, though he's done no wrong.

He picks up a program and sits near the back. While he waits for things to get underway, his clarinet professor sits beside him.

"Jack!" he says. "Congratulations."

A forced smile.

"Any guests with you today?"

Jack gets the impression his clarinet professor is unaware of his current troubles. "No, my mother had to change her plans."

"I see," the clarinet professor says. "Well, I'm glad I caught you, because I heard about an opportunity that might interest you. The Chicago Symphony is in a bit of a slump these days, like most performing arts organizations in this recession."

Jack nods, watching two men lift a podium onto the stage.

"They've cut back in shows, and are looking for cheaper events to run. The managing director has a new summer initiative. They're showcasing new composers by playing their works— world premieres if you will. The composers don't get much compensation, which is how the organization saves money, but the publicity is certainly worthwhile to the composers. After all, this is the Chicago Symphony we're talking about."

The two men on stage drape a U of M sash over the podium. "Definitely worthwhile," Jack says.

"So, and I hope you won't be mad, I sent in your symphony score a few weeks ago. They're interested in talking to you in person."

Jack's head abruptly snaps to the right, facing his clarinet professor. "You sent in my work?"

The clarinet professor nods. "Is that alright? I think they'll choose you. What's more attractive to spice up a recession than a fresh young talent, all of twenty-two, ready to launch his new promising career?"

But Jack isn't so certain about his talents, considering the subject of his symphony ran away. All the same, he answers, "Yes, thank you. I could get down to Chicago."

"I'll check in with them, see if I can get a meeting arranged," his professor says. "Consider it your graduation gift."

An hour later, Jack is walking back to his temporary home, hard-earned diploma in hand, thinking about the days ahead.

CHAPTER 9

Pam Mekinski is planting gladioli: pointy-side up, fertilizer over each bulb, soil, water. She plants three careful rows, alternating red and yellow along the way. The bulbs are soundless as they nestle into the dirt: fertilizer, soil, water, pat pat pat, wipe brow, dig in pail, start again. The routine sounds exactly the same to observers, except the time Pam accidentally puts two bulbs in one hole, the second tumbling down the little dirt hill. The bulbs meet with the faintest smack, but the birds above take notice, rubbing their beaks together.

Pam's goal is to hide the tacky fake wood look on the front of her trailer with blooms. She refers to the fake wood as "faux bois" to laugh off her poorness. The official start of summer is still a few weeks away, but Jack's mother must start work early in the morning as the Midwest humidity is particularly raw this year, nearly shredding the afternoons to bits.

And though it's still spring, it might be a touch too late to plant bulbs, Pam considers. They might not open up until late September, and then what's the point? But the methodical work feels nice, the carefulness feels calming. When the kids were little, Pam would spend many long hours in the garden, their laughs and cries and fights and curiosities all rows away from her, blooms and petals and dirt piles away from her. Being a single mother was impossibly hard. It felt nice to be alone in the garden back then. It still does. Of course, the mind wanders while gardening, and sometimes that's unproductive. Because work slows down, however menial and seasonal, when you think of your husband who wandered off, who was never seen again after a particularly mouthy and violent fight. The kids, fatherless. Work, important or not even close, seems unnecessary when you're living in a plastic tube without a reliable fridge or regularly cleaned linens. Pam won a free night at the Holiday Inn a few winters back through a church raffle. It was better than an island getaway, Pam decided, and she continued to sneak back in for months after to sit in the steamy whirlpool for a few minutes when the second shift workers were busy handing things over to the night folks.

And yet, Pam is acutely aware that she doesn't deserve any better than this. As a rabbit creeps out from behind her neighbor's trailer, its eyes pulsing, its body nervously straining forward, Pam picks up her spade. As the rabbit darts across her yard, she hurls the spade and takes off a chunk of his fur and flesh, a little blood running down the rabbit's hind leg as he makes a pained call. "I didn't know rabbits made noise," Pam muses.

As she returns to gardening proper, her warped screen door flings open and Jeremy hustles out. His feet move swiftly down the old steps, his eyes on the pavement of the road ahead. "Off to do my route, Ma," he calls, pulling his bike to a stand. Pam's eyes look upward, noticing the blue-gray clouds, feeling the atmosphere getting sticky.

"It'll rain before you're done. Want to use my car today? There's gas in it."

Jeremy doesn't respond, instead pedaling toward the main drag that'll lead him into town, where people can afford things like newspaper subscriptions. Where, strangely, a lot of people still actually look forward to getting their paper, because they're comfortable in life, and can relax with the Arts section in their lap. Town people, especially those who live around the university, like Mae Harrington.

"Whatever," says Pam, getting her hands dirty once more. As she works, her mind drifts to Jack, who actually invited her but then quickly uninvited her to his graduation. She hasn't seen Jack in years, doesn't even know what her son looks like anymore, isn't sure where he's headed next. Pam knows that slut he lives with probably made Jack take back his offer to let her stay there. She was even going to make a carrot cake for the occasion.

*

In town, Jeremy starts practicing again. Lately he's been imaging the worst things he can think of, things too terrible to imagine for more than a few seconds, so that if he should actually come across such a scene, or perhaps even cause such a scene, he won't lose focus because he'll have already experienced it. Things like cute chubby toddlers being backed over by garbage trucks, a church roof collapsing during a big wedding ceremony, atomic bombs blowing off his hands like dandelion seeds and spreading the world over, boom boom boom. Things that no person, priest, or prophet could fix. He needs to let his mind explore these scenes, embrace these possibilities, let it all feel natural.

He throws a paper into some shrubs on Grant Street. Subscriptions have fallen a bit since he started his route, but those who remain are passionate about their printed news from New York and London and shit out of Libya even though a computer is speedier at delivering news than some moody teenager with ink on his hands and trouble in his brain. He stops just short of Mae's house, as he often does, to study her property, imagine her life, and think of his brother. Sometimes he gets to watch one or both, see them fade in and out of rooms, wafting around like smoke, talking to each other once in a while. He'd love to hear their conversations, love to know which words they use to describe their days, how they phrase difficult questions, avoid or attack love. But she's gone now, and Jack will probably follow.

*

"Folks we're about ten minutes from our stop in Chicago. Please make sure you take all of your belongings with you."

I awake in my seat on the Greyhound. Out my window, the Chicago skyline is visible and strong, lining up on the back of the looping Skyway. I haven't been here for five years, but with Lake Michigan to the east, and the Cubbies to the north, and the Sox to the south, I won't lose my way. Buildings change in the middle, businesses come and go, but Chicago remains the same city I've always come back to.

We unload on Harrison Street. Passengers stretch and pull their luggage and garment bags together, collecting headphones and magazines. Most step off the bus and into the arms of loved ones, or old friends, or college roommates. I make a quick exit and head toward the heart of downtown. I'm about a fifteen-minute walk from where I'd hoped to start my reunion, the Magnificent Mile, which happens to be Michigan Avenue. I pat my handbag, now a subconscious effort to check for Jack's gun. I realize, as the bag makes a metal clanging noise, that parts of St. Paul are still in there too, like the door lock and a bit of the door's frame. I'm careless to carry this so freely, and will have to find a new home for this evidence soon.

The grass off the sidewalk is wet, dark green patches bleeding with trailing footsteps. I look to the overcast sky, wondering if we're in for severe weather. I don't have an umbrella or even proper outerwear. Beside me, people pass swiftly in trench coats and jean jackets, carrying insulated coffees with steaming tops. Shoes squeak and chirp like canaries. Street signs glisten and pop with color. I wonder if the river boat tours, showing off Chicago's architecture and telling the city's history, are canceled for tonight.

My daydreaming carries me all the way to Michigan Avenue, where I'm now steps away from the art museum I've always enjoyed. I heard an ad on the bus driver's radio for the museum, boasting free admission today until 8 PM. That's about all that happened on the bus ride before I fell asleep. It was all quiet, and uneventful; the best I hoped for.

The line is long, but people-watching makes the wait swift. There's a group of mothers with their children, probably on an organized outing for a playgroup. The mothers have pale skin, and pastel tops, and large diamond rings. There's a father with his son; they look Jewish. A solo traveler is reading a Chicago guidebook, occasionally looking up to monitor the line's progress. His backpack is full, and his glasses are thick. An elderly couple leans on one another, smiling despite the hard cement beneath their thin shoes. Behind us, cars crawl past, bikes glide between sedans, and the intermittent metro buses puff to a stop.

Soon it's my turn and I'm welcomed inside. I stand in the foyer looking for a metal detector. Suspecting I'm safe, I head toward the coatroom. I'm tempted to leave my handbag behind, gun and all, but feel I should handle the situation properly, at least taking the time to wipe my fingerprints and clear out my needed personal belongings. And so, I proceed instead to the main galleries, ready for my night out with a little extra hardware in tow.

I recall certain pieces from the Indian and Southeast Asian galleries and paintings in the Impressionist galleries. And there's something quirky yet strangely engaging about the paperweight collection, tucked away into the lowest and furthest corner of the building. Each glass paperweight is handmade, with incredibly intricate designs inside, such swirling colors and difficult patterns. Some took the artists a year or more of daily work to get right. For a fun paperweight, and a tiny decoration at that. I'm startled by the commitment of others to their craft. Of course, this all makes me think of Jack and his clarinet.

I sift through the rooms, brushing shoulders and hips and elbows with the huge throngs of people here. We're on an invisible conveyor belt, moving over the parquet wood floor in unison. Some break the line to step forward if a particular piece catches their eye. A woman in red has done so to examine ancient pottery found in Israel. Her eyes tell a story of intrigue and disbelief. Her breathing is shallow and she quickly moves onto similar pieces found in the dig, stitching together a time long ago.

Later I'm at the double doors of a special exhibit. It's quiet in here, reverent in here. There are spotlights from the ceiling, shining at angles onto the tall walls. A sign proclaims, *Yousuf Karsh: Regarding Heroes*. A man slides to the left and I see a portrait of Audrey Hepburn, looking sleek and concave. While still beautiful, there is an unrelenting sadness about her. Both her posture and her expression are slightly remorseful, though delicately so. If she came alive out of her photograph, she would be frail, and demure, and maybe secretive.

There are stunning portraits everywhere, of celebrities, politicians, scientists, dreamers, thinkers. I gaze at Frank Lloyd Wright, George Bernard Shaw, and Dwight Eisenhower. Somehow, Karsh managed to capture these Goliaths in a way I've never seen presented before, that perhaps the world has never seen before. Each photo holds a surprise, a view of each person that was previously unknown. Why does Georgia O'Keefe seem troubled? Why does Jacqueline Kennedy look so shy? There are faces and bodies and personalities everywhere, all well-known, but strangers in this light.

I'm reminded of my Apostles at St. Paul's. I think of Peter, looking so out of place, yet so familiar.

A group gathers around Albert Einstein's portrait. A deep sense of contentment is awash on Albert's face, his hands folded under his chin in a prayer-like hold. Karsh has written the following about Einstein:

"At Princeton's Institute for Advanced Study, I found Einstein a simple, kindly, almost childlike man, too great for any of the postures of eminence. One did not have to understand his science to feel the power of his mind or the force of his personality. He spoke sadly, yet serenely, as one who had looked into the universe, far past mankind's small affairs. When I asked him what the world would be like were another atomic bomb to be dropped, he replied wearily, 'Alas, we will no longer be able to hear the music of Mozart.'"

A student standing next to me grunts his approval.

As the sun sets over the museum, patrons file out, looking for their dinners and their next bit of stimulation. A security guard wanders around the main hall, nodding his goodnights and glancing into exhibit rooms. I again find myself patting my handbag, knowing I have to get rid of the accessory inside.

He comes right up to me, his body a little scrappy, his smile unusually wide. He doesn't possess the necessary swagger for his job; in fact, he looks dangerously harmless, and actually, pretty enchanting. I like his soft brown hair and square glasses. I like his pale skin, his hazel eyes, and aura of kindness, of goodness. "Did you have a nice time?" he asks earnestly.

I think I may be blushing. "I did. Thank you."

I walk through the foyer and into the night air, turning around to catch one last glance of the first person in a decade whom I've been attracted to before I go.

It's now a perfect blend of warm and cool outside. I head down the sidewalk and make my way toward the parks. Soon I'm standing on a wooden pier at the edge of Lake Michigan. There are several fishing boats and a yacht in the water. I see couples and a few families down the bank, but there's no one around me. After multiple nervous looks in all directions, spinning in full, slow circles, I slip the gun out into the open. Using a fresh tissue and glasses cleaner I happened to find in my handbag on the bus, I wipe the revolver clean, though I doubt I'm doing much to protect myself. Then, with one last nervous peek around me, I step onto the pier and hurl the gun as far as I can. It lands with a moderate splash and disappears under the surface. I'm certain that one day, a swimmer or jogger or even a child will happen upon the gun as the tides bring it to the shore. And I realize, as the boats peacefully bop over the waves, by the time the discovery is made, my fate for using the gun in the first place will probably be complete. I'll either have paid a fine, or sat in jail, or sunk down to Hell. On my way out of the park, I tip my handbag over a public trash can, glass and metal fragments falling to the bottom with a sharp bang.

Finally.

I decide to spend the night in the Congress Hotel, just a short walk from here. I recall the weeknight rates being quite reasonable, likely because the "historic" hotel has seen better days. The narrow hallways are dim, the heavily upholstered rooms seem damp. But you can't beat the location, right on the Magnificent Mile and steps away from wonder after wonder. On my way over, I see a sign in a gift shop window proclaiming: *Chicago T-shirts—2 for $10!*

What a steal. I step inside, buy clothes, snacks, and a light dinner. My appetite, once so ravenous, diminishes the further I slide into this predicament. And my energy levels are really tumbling along with my outlook. Rest can't come soon enough.

*

Jack is walking through the house one last time before heading down to Chicago. Like Mae always was, he's nervous about leaving the house unattended. He's unplugged everything, locked all the windows, cleared the answering machine, but still, leaving this time feels different, more serious.

As he grabs a spring jacket out of the front closet, Oscar strolls up to his legs. "Oh, the cat," Jack says, sighing with frustration. He starts picturing neighbors in his head, wondering whom he should ask for help. The doorbell breaks his planning.

Mae's usual paperboy stands behind the door. "Hi there," he says.

"Hello, Jeremy," Jack replies. "What is it?"

Jeremy extends a clipboard. "It's time to renew," he says coldly. Jack begins filling out the form and says, "Jeremy, I need a favor."

The paperboy raises his eyebrows, looking interested. "Oh?"

"I'll be out for the next few days. If I leave you a key, could you come in and feed the cat? You'll be here every day anyway, right?"

Jeremy nods. "Not a problem."

"Really?" Jack says, relieved. "Thanks for being cool about this. Mom doesn't have to know."

The door closes. But Jeremy remains on the stoop, holding a key, amazed at his luck.

CHAPTER 10

Morning on Hickory Street. This part of town feels like the pearl necklace of Chicago, curving gently and beautifully around stately brick townhouses and upscale cafés. A man is edging his yard with the precision of an engineer, creating a perfect quarter-inch gap between the grass and the sidewalk. Flowering bushes abound, some surpassing the height of first story windows. Pricey cars are neatly parked on the side of the road, mostly imports. There's a sweetness in the air, perhaps homemade cinnamon rolls swelling in an oven or croissants browning under a housewife's watchful eye. Everything is just so here.

I'm lost in contrasting thought as usual when I happen upon a group of people entering a house. A sign is perched in the yard that reads: "Estate Sale. One day only. All welcome." I've only been to one estate sale. It was small, but I found matching lamps that I liked. It's hard to find a decent lamp set. They're often too formal or too tacky.

I make my way up the walk behind a businessman carrying a leather briefcase. He removes a pen from his pocket and clicks it to life, marking down notes on a tablet. Maybe he's from an auction house. Or a real estate company. People come to estate sales for lots of reasons.

Soon I'm in a formal sitting room, with heavy burgundy curtains and satin striped couches. Every item boasts a white price tag, even the rug I'm standing on, even the light switch covers. I quietly mill around with the rest of the shoppers, inspecting the front sides and back sides of objects, admiring the former owner's tastes. The decision to hold an estate sale is surely a difficult one for families to make. Selling everything a deceased family member owns is sort of like cutting off ties with a former friend. Except days later, strangers troop through the house, handling everything with or without care that used to be important. Sometimes sentimental items are spared from the shoppers, but not always. I suppose it depends on the closeness of the family, just like so many affairs in life depend on the closeness of relationships. How I wish I could be independent, free of relationships, but no one can be. No one.

The sitting room spills into a cheery kitchen, with white cupboards and bold splashes of color. Again, there are price tags wrapped around each object, even the faucet. Perhaps this family is in hard times, or perhaps they want no memory of what remains. I examine dishes and cookware, flatware and coffee mugs. There is chatter and moments of excitement. It's a very nice house, with very nice belongings. With prices starting at fifty cents, it's better than hitting a mega sale at a department store, and certainly more classy than a garage sale.

I'm pondering taking a few teacups when I notice a crowd of people gathering in a sunroom. Their faces are sullen, their eyes distant. It's quiet, and strange in that room. I make my way over, eager to see what's developing.

The room overlooks a vibrant backyard garden, dense and active with lilies and hydrangeas. A group steps back and I get a view of the unfolding interest. There are rows and rows of paintings set into racks, mostly watercolors, some oil. Ships on the lake, roses, a coastal village, horses, children, sunrises, sunsets. There are many subjects, many sizes, many moods. I approach a rack and gingerly flip through the works, admiring some for their brightness, others for their darkness. Hundreds of pieces are up for examination this morning. The price tags here are all the same: $10.

I'm particularly drawn to a painting of a house, shown under a rustic streetlight and a bit in the distance. The house is old, but well cared for. A rock stepping path meanders through the grass to the cottage door, quaint and inviting. A silhouette of a tabby is in the glowing front window. I feel homesick.

The artist has carefully signed her name in the corner of each piece: *Abby*, elegant and strong. I wonder if this extensive collection is from a local artist, if Abby lives in Chicago. Perhaps she has a studio downtown.

A sharply dressed black man steps up beside me, his eyes resting on the house painting.

"It's very charismatic," he says.

I agree. "It's perfect. Do you know if the artist is local? Does she have a studio around here? I'd like to meet her."

The man raises his eyebrows at me, standing quite still. "This is the deceased homeowner's work. The estate sale was billed in the paper as an artist's sale."

A pain washes over me unlike any I've felt in recent times, crushing me from the outside in. How did I not realize?

"All of these paintings? All of them were . . . Abby's? And she's the woman who lived here?"

The man nods, looking at me with interest and pity. I understand the somberness of the room now. Hundreds of paintings, her life work, all done with such care, and all for sale for just $10, post-mortem. "I'm guessing this is her full collection," he says.

The sunroom's windows shake with confirmation.

Dreams unrealized. She probably completed most of these

pieces in this very space, with pleasant views and cups of spiced tea. I want to take the house painting. I want to take them all, find places and platforms to show this stranger's talents. Again I think of her family, and wonder if any of her creations were removed and saved. For prosperity, or even admiration. Relationships.

My eyes sting. My legs are heavy. I reach for the house painting, carefully tucking it under my arm.

"It makes me pretty sad, too," the man tells me. His face is gentle. We accompany each other through the remaining rooms, occasionally discussing an item of note. Everything seems less wonderful now. This isn't a good sale anymore; it's someone's life, being sold away in a morning. I find myself inconsolable over the matter the longer I'm in the house, even finding the once charming teacups too much to bear. Finally we've returned to the front door, where a makeshift cashier stand is waiting. I pay for the painting, unsmiling, and am relieved to get outdoors, where the air is crisp and the mourning house is at my back. The man remains at my side.

"Feel like getting a cup of coffee?" he says.

I don't feel uncomfortable by his offer. Our age difference must be close to thirty years, and we had some polite and harmless conversations as we soldiered through the former owner's home. I'm sure he's just got an open morning.

"Sure," I reply.

"The name's Frank," he tells me, reaching out his wrinkling hand.

I forget I'm hiding. "I'm Mae," I state.

The house settles and sighs at their backs, the roof dancing under the day's increasing heat, the grass whispering about the pair as they grow smaller and smaller down the road.

*

Three blocks away from the coffee shop where Frank and Mae are sitting, each enjoying an espresso drink and muffin, Jack is parking his car in a public garage. He has a meeting in a few hours with the Chicago Symphony. He'll need to find a decent place for lunch, and to change into a dress shirt and tie. Jack isn't too sure what to expect from this meeting. Likely, paperwork, and hopefully, he'll get to listen to the orchestra play his piece sometime before it's performed for an audience. He told himself on the ride over that he can't be "one of those" composers; he can't demand that every crescendo and decrescendo and tempo change conform to his precise standards. He can't tell the orchestra or the director what to do, being a rookie, being given such an opportunity. He'll look at the experience as a learning opportunity, and a springboard, and try to enjoy his time in Chicago, too.

Mae always spoke so highly of Chicago. Jack knows she has a history with this city, and because of this, his eyes and mind are open wider than usual today. Everything is of interest right now: the people, the buildings, the sounds, the vibe. Each store's window gallery gets a careful look from Jack, who is also assessing pizza shops on corners. When in Rome, he thinks.

It's after his pizza lunch, a quick change in the Elk Lodge's public restrooms, and a saunter down the street and into his meeting that he's finally taken aback, finally startled after the strange and heavy week he's endured. Everything is just so incredibly odd right now, so foreign right now. He's sitting at a long wooden table, carefully reviewing a contract when the Symphony House Manager walks in and says, "We're glad you came down today. We'd like to perform your piece this Friday."

Jack's head snaps up from the legal work. "This Friday? As in, a few days from now?"

The house manager nods. "We're all ready to advertise. And the orchestra is ready to go. Out of all of the submissions, the musicians liked your piece the most."

Jack feels the panic of a nervous soloist, even though he'll have a seat in the hall. "Were you going to contact me and let me know?" he says.

"Tried to. Seems your phone line is out of order."

Jack feels sick.

"Anyway, there's a full dress rehearsal soon. We'll put you up in a hotel. I hope you can stick around?"

Jack agrees, though at this point he has to.

*

I'm walking west with Frank now. We sat in the coffee shop for over three hours, talking a bit about the city, but mostly about our personal lives. Somehow I lost the desire to remain anonymous, perhaps because of the intimate experience we shared at the estate sale. In addition to my name, he knows that I live in Ann Arbor and that I teach at the university. He also knows that my parents died in a car accident just before I started college, and that I've never been married. It does actually feel good to have a new friend, get a fresh start, though speaking so candidly right now is unwise.

Turns out Frank is a former professor. He just retired from the University of Chicago where he taught American History for decades. We compared war stories and it seems the life of a professor checks out the same anywhere: some good semesters, some awful semesters. Ongoing battles with the administration. Students who inspire and students who make us think about leaving our jobs. Weird issues with colleagues, strange graduate students. Happy times during sabbaticals, funny stories about visiting professors.

Frank abruptly stops walking. "Well, I'm home," he says, nodding toward a nicely kept Cape Cod house. It's white with blue trim. I can picture him hauling out a push mower and starting an afternoon of yard work. "I'd invite you in for coffee, but I suppose we've had our fill," he says, smiling warmly.

I thank him all the same. "Say, where are you staying?" he wonders. "Close by?"

I tell him I'm at the Congress Hotel. "Ah. Well, a bit of a haul, but if you feel like coming around for dinner, you're more than welcome to. In fact, please do." I thank him for his generous offer and tell him I'll stop by if I can.

And with that, I'm heading back toward the lake to people watch and exhale at Millennium Park.

*

After Mae leaves, Frank turns the deadbolt lock and really perks up, excited about his new unexpected mission. A small pug dog wriggles before him, hopping up and down for attention. "Hi, Sally," Frank says, patting the dog on the head. Sally speeds off into the kitchen, hoping for her standard He's Home treat.

But Frank has other matters on his mind. He tosses his hat on the kitchen table and starts down the hall. The floorboards start their familiar singing. His house was built nearly one hundred years ago, and while it's getting noisier, nothing leaks, and all the original carpentry work is still standing. Frank considers this pretty darned good. Plus, the extensive crown molding adds a lot of character, and the wooden floors still shine beautifully. It's not a house he'll ever part with easily.

His office is at the end of the hallway. He's long reminded himself that it's now a "study" since retirement, but since his desk is still stacked with work, it isn't a study yet. There are journal publications to review and even more to submit. It's been a busy retirement, and his friends worry for him. But he doesn't want to think about stopping work altogether. What would be left? Merely taking Sally for an evening walk? Filling chairs in coffee shops?

Hardly seems like a fulfilling, productive life for an active gentle-man.

Franks turns on his computer and scans his mail pile while he waits for the machine to boot. He's had a few offers to deliver guest lectures lately, and he may go ahead and accept one. Gotta keep the mental gears oiled, he reminds himself. There's an offer from the University of Colorado that sounds particularly enticing. Can't beat the scenic beauty. Wouldn't hurt to climb a mountain or two, maybe let Sally bound down some hiking trails.

The computer is ready. Frank launches his email program and scrolls through this week's messages, looking for a note he read a few days back. An email from an old colleague is titled: "What they're doing in Michigan."

Frank clicks on the subject line and the full correspondence pops onto the screen.

"Had to forward this on," his friend wrote. "Apparently some Michigan professor is having a little something-something with her student. Nothing newsworthy there, except that she has a thing for breaking into churches, and is now armed and on the run. What a way to spend summer vacation! Why didn't we think of that?"

The email contains a link to the local news story out of Ann Arbor. Frank clicks the link and waits. "Error: Story not found." So, he takes to Google, doing some searching for this wanted pro-fessor. There's very little out there except the briefest of recaps. He can't even find her name. Maybe it was a hoax. Or maybe they've already caught her and this is all old news now.

Frank thinks about his new friend Mae. She's very intelligent and vibrant, but something seems amiss. She was nervous during their coffee break, and seemed distracted, almost pained. Perhaps she truly is just visiting the town and the estate sale bothered her on a fundamental level. It was terribly sad to see someone's life work for sale for ten bucks a pop. And Frank was a stranger. Everyone acts a little oddly when meeting someone for the first time, when presenting themselves to someone new.

Sally clips into the room, dragging her leash. Frank supposes this matter will remain unresolved unless Mae shows up for dinner.

*

The streets of Ann Arbor are absorbing an amber hue as the sun starts tipping down and the buildings create long shadows. In residential areas, fathers are pulling into driveways after their day at the office, and sprinklers are springing to life behind hedgerows. And on Mae Harrington's stoop, her paperboy Jeremy is inserting a key into the front door.

Jeremy's had this route for five years. He started when he was a sophomore in high school, looking to earn extra money for weed and really solid metal music. He doesn't know anything about any of his customers, except of course a bit about Mae, because her increasingly bizarre behavior forced him to take notice, and oh yeah, his brother shacks up with her. She was usually polite, often working in her yard with a warm smile when it was paper time. But over the last few months, she began looking at him with unusual concern, almost suspicion. Sometimes it appeared Mae was actually waiting for him, studying him, hunting him from behind her garbage bins or her oak tree. Now that she was a fugitive and the talk of the town, a celebrity of sorts for Ann Arbor, Jeremy feels a sick thrill walking over her floors and carpets, scanning her personal items with swelling interest.

After a quick stop in the kitchen to feed the cat, Jeremy heads upstairs, eager to see Mae's bedroom. It smells soft and feminine, and the airy feel is comforting. A few outer space photos line her dresser, and he pauses to examine the shots. Why space? Does she want to be an astronaut or something? Surely the police have been in this room a lot, going over Mae's things and looking for clues about her behavior. The general consensus is that Mae has a true and fierce obsession for religion, but how far will she go? What are the voices in her head urging her to do? Jeremy knows the type, having hung around potheads and punk thrashers. But obviously Mae is a little too refined and smart to fit into those groups. She might be the real fucking deal, really fucking crazy.

It doesn't feel altogether right to stand in this room, but Jeremy goes further and starts opening drawers. This could be a dead woman's room. Some locals think she ran off to kill herself. She doesn't have any kids, doesn't have a family. No known siblings. Never married. Parents are apparently out of the picture. And not much in these drawers, Jeremy notices. Some sweaters and jeans. A few pairs of knit socks. And one small round . . . cracker? Jeremy's not sure, and tries to pry the little scrap out of the corner. But it's not coming up, and the longer he tries, the warmer his hands feel, almost hot, nearly itching, like a sudden skin allergy, or like fiberglass seeping into his skin.

He pulls back in pain, rubbing his hand and worried that some cop or detective could rush in here. Maybe the whole place is being monitored, and someone is about to pull up. But he's fascinated, sickly so.

Before he leaves he stands a moment at Mae's bedside, wondering what sort of lewd acts have gone on between her and Jack. Jeremy has never fucked a girl in his life, has never spent the night away from the trailer, can't even imagine the easy life Jack now has. As he thinks about all this, his muscles tense and a slow rage lights up his body. "Fuck him. Fucking bastard," Jeremy says, stomping out of the house. If Mae were there, she might catch a glimpse of his tail, whipping mightily this way and that.

CHAPTER 11

Captain Douglas flips through a brown leather scrapbook that was removed from Mae Harrington's dresser, found alongside a little stack of Communion wafers. Mae apparently put the book together the summer after high school graduation, but there aren't any happy memories documented. It seems this scrapbook was completed by order of a therapist. The first page has a wonderful candid photo of Mae's parents, two very nice looking folks, laughing while walking through a snowy park. The next page has a newspaper clipping with the headline: "Family outing turns tragic."

Captain Douglas has read the clipping a dozen times now, thinking heavily about the circumstances, wondering how deeply this is still affecting Mae. The family car was crossing a tall icy bridge over water, the kind of bridge made from uneven wooden planks on thick wooden posts. The bridge almost seems coastal, like it could support a seaside pier amusement park, like foamy ocean waves should swirl underneath. But this is Michigan, not California. In the summer, it's the kind of bridge you'd slow down for and bump over. In the winter, the car Mae was driving with her parents as passengers slid into the rail after she heard a plank snap. The rail broke, and the car went. Mae survived. Her parents did not. Making the situation more gravely depressing, surreally so, was a girl ice skating at the time of the accident. According to Mae, the girl screamed and slid into the water when the car shredded the ice-covered surface. The girl drowned, too.

The rest of the scrapbook contains bits and pieces of her parents' life, as well as interesting commentary from Mae. "None of this is my fault," she writes, she reminds herself, on several of the particularly dark pages. "That girl is a beautiful angel in Heaven," she notes on a page showing a school photo of the ice skater. It's just an intensely depressing scrapbook, the kind most people would want tucked away into an attic for eternity. Mae kept it in a drawer within arm's reach of her bed.

Survivor's guilt. A winter accident rewritten as murder in her brain. Over the years, she's actually convinced herself that she purposefully killed her parents—and Mae wants holy forgiveness to right this mess. Women like Mae Harrington aren't killers. But survivor's guilt, in unstable minds, is as dangerous as an icy bridge. Or the gun Mae stole and used to blow open a locked church door.

Just a month prior to Mae's life turning point, another girl, sitting in the back seat of her aunt's car, went over that rail, too. Her name is Betty. She's in a wheelchair now, but manages to run a sweet little coffee shop a few towns over. Betty makes a mean lemon merengue pie, a recipe she inherited from her aunt, who didn't survive. That was a real bad winter. Captain Douglas stands to stretch when his phone jumps to life. "Yeah?" he answers.

"So, the professor case. We found the church's missing cross, in the pond by her house."

"Shut up," he says. "In the goddamn pond?"

"That's correct."

"So she must have dragged that thing all the way down. . ." he voice trails off.

"What is it?"

Captain Douglas considers his words carefully. "Did you do a full sweep of the pond?"

"Like with a camera? No, it's too murky for that. What are we looking for?"

"Then you're going to have to drain it," the Captain says, "just in case she unloaded anything else there," he finishes, tracing his finger over the photo of the young ice skater.

Too worked up to just sit and wait, the Captain nearly gallops down to his squad car. Showing up at the pond right now would definitely be overbearing, would certainly piss a few people off, but doing a little double-check down at campus seems perfectly fine. Campus is much closer to the pond anyway, should he be needed.

*

The English Department is on the fourth floor of the Humanities building. The investigators were already around this way, but Captain Douglas was unimpressed by their work. "Her colleagues all had the same general commentary," it said on the summary sheet. "Mae is diligent. Mae keeps a routine. Mae is professional. Mae doesn't share a lot about her personal life. No, they didn't know she was renting a room to her student."

The Captain walks into the office area, where the department secretary is arranging student files. "Hi, ma'am, Captain Douglas from the Detroit Station. We spoke on the phone?" he says warmly and calmly, knowing this is just the type of situation that makes others edgy and uncomfortable.

"Yes, I recall," she says, definitely sounding tense. "Did you want the keys to her office, like the others did?"

The Captain looks down at the secretary's papers. "If you could open her door for me, that'd be great. Oh and Jack's file, if you have it handy," he says with forced cheer. No need to pull out the warrant card and badge or anything, he reminds himself. The secretary slides a short stack of papers his way before leading him down the hall. There isn't much in Jack's papers: his transcripts show he's never gotten below an "A" in any class, which is pretty remarkable in its own right, but more so for a kid without a support system. And it dawns on Captain Douglas: maybe that's why Mae and Jack were drawn to each other, for neither one has much of anyone.

"Just let me know when you're finished," the secretary says after she opens Mae's office door, probably relieved to get away from the tall man in blue.

Captain Douglas enters and immediately turns on his tape recorder. "Sparse, like her home," he says while pulling on gloves. "Well organized. No personal photos, just a poster of . . ." he trails off to inspect a calendar pinned to the wall. "Just old summer tour dates for the Counting Crows." He tips his head at this.

He starts pulling drawers open in the metal desk, the same industrial-grade metal desk that every staff member on this campus is issued. "Office supplies. Syllabus stacks. A medical dictionary. One of those costume jewelry whale tail necklaces."

Upon hearing this, the young maple sapling outside of Mae's window, the one that Mae looks at so lovingly, wondering when it will grow big enough to place a bench underneath, stands on its tiptoe roots and strains to hear the rest of his list.

Inside, the Captain finishes rooting through Mae's light possessions. "Chapstick. Tea bags. And . . ." Here he feels excitement, validity. "And more Communion wafers."

The sapling nods, not surprised in the least by this finding, then lowers itself back down for an afternoon in the sun.

*

The strings are tuning, wonderful screeches mixing and blending on stage. Jack sits in the hall, a clipboard on his lap. Both the conductor and the Symphony manager have urged Jack to make critiques. "It's your work, after all, and there'll be a question and answer session with you for the papers at some point," they told him. Though Jack has recorded all the parts by themselves on his clarinet, he's never heard his symphony performed properly, by live musicians. It's a tense anticipation.

Like many symphonies, Jack stuck to the standard four-movement form. And though they don't have to be named, Jack has issued names to each movement. After a lot of back and forth, they were labeled: *Imagination, Un-bride, Porcelain, Gone*. Naming the overall symphony was the most difficult part. For a while, *Symphony No. 1* was sufficient. Eventually, *Mae's Turn* took its place. It's also the name that's currently displayed on the venue's outside marquee, making this whole matter all the more real.

Soon enough, all of the bows are resting, and all of the musicians are still, including a male vocalist standing at the edge of the stage. The conductor turns to acknowledge Jack, a formality that will likely occur tomorrow night, too. Jack realizes he'll have to find a tux rental shop, and perhaps find some acid reflux medicine for this strange and permanent stress. And with that, the conductor raises his arms, and the cellos sing the low, swirling sounds of Jack's opening.

The symphony is just over an hour long when performed at Jack's tempo markings, and is meant to be played without an intermission. There haven't been any pauses in Jack and Mae's life, so why would there be in the musical rendition, Jack reasoned. As the work progresses, Jack remembers the real-life plot points that made for such clear sections of the music. He is particularly moved by the oboe's interpretation of summer nights in the backyard, the crickets and fancy tablecloth picnics, and dipping their toes in the water. Like they were a real couple, stitching together warm memories to carry them through another Michigan winter. But as Jack hears it, listens to the music tell the story, the memory seems one-sided now. One pining lover, one unique but clearly disinterested older woman. It hurts Jack to hear, but there is an undeniable captured accuracy he's proud of, no matter the pain. And he remembers, like watching a home video in his mind, the pier he promised to fix but never finished.

And just like that, the symphony ends. All eyes turn to Jack, waiting patiently for some sort of approval in the half-lit hall. Jack remains still. He looks down at his clipboard, where no notes are written. After a moment, the conductor clears his throat. Finally, Jack stands. "I loved it. Thank you." And then, a moment of surprise.

"Jack, would you like to play it with us tomorrow night? We have a clarinet you could use."

*

It's just after five. I'm retracing the way back to Frank's home, hoping he's around tonight. It's been a quiet day, mostly spent reading in my room. I've decided to leave tomorrow. To go back home to Ann Arbor. To face consequences, sort things out, see what's repairable and what's not. It's been a short but interesting visit to Chicago, but I understand I can't avoid difficulties forever. Plus, my immediate cash supply is running thin. I'm not entirely sure why going back to Frank's seems important, but it does. As soon as I left him, I knew I'd accept his invitation to come back. Perhaps because Frank feels trustworthy, despite our lack of history. He seems wise and careful, someone fresh to interact with. I'm also rather envious of his life; newly retired, living in a quaint Chicago home with only a happy dog to answer to. It's easy enough to fantasize about starting over by examining Frank's success and contentedness. For a while, for one more dinner, I can pretend I already have started over.

I ring his bell, empty-handed. I considered picking up a bottle of wine or a loaf of bread, but decided against it. Also, he really might not be expecting me, and he might not even be home, either. And if he is home, he probably hasn't prepared too much in advance, since one can't count on the reliability of strangers. Basically, I don't know what will unfold, but it feels nice all the same.

As the door opens, the smell of ham and biscuits and green beans greets me, along with the joy of Frank, who is positively beaming. "Mae!" he says, gesturing me inside. As I step into the foyer, his small giddy dog that I heard about over coffee makes wide running circles around the room. I think of Jack, and my cat, and hope the two are keeping each other company back in Ann Arbor.

"Do you cook like this for yourself every night?" I ask him while removing my shoes.

He chuckles. "Well, I was hoping you'd come back. So I went all out, telling myself that if you were a no-show, then what the hell, I'd still get quite a meal."

I smile appreciatively and walk over to the table. "Looks like it's all ready then?" Frank confirms and I sit, admiring his nice table settings. It seems Frank has done quite well for himself. I offered plenty of my background yesterday, but heard little about Frank's side of life.

I clear my throat. "So sorry to ask bluntly in case this brings up a sore spot, but is there a Mrs. Frank here I should greet, too?"

Frank shakes his head. "Nope, never was. I'm rather particular about everything. Best to wing it on my own, I always think."

And with that, we start serving ourselves.

Frank is hiding his agenda well. Banking on Mae's return, he had a nice conversation with a Detroit Captain this afternoon, who confirmed that yes, she's still missing. Frank reiterated that he's "not sure," but that the professor "just might be in town," and is "perhaps coming back for dinner" if the police want to do any surveillance. And just a bit earlier, Frank couldn't help but notice two squad cars outside his home. Soon the officers were replaced with an unmarked car and a plainly dressed man, who took up the best spot on the street, right across from his door, and has remained there since. So they're not alone at this point, though Frank is not expecting the FBI to come crashing through the windows. The Detroit Captain assured Frank that this is an "observation" measure, and that he should carry on as normally as possible.

Frank, however, would like to confirm her identity and get more dirt. Short of occasionally kicking some serious ass down at the bowling lanes on 34th Street, this is his biggest adrenaline rush in quite some time. After both plates are full and forks are moving, Franks opens up the conversation. "So you said you teach at the university. Do you have any summer courses, or are you off until the fall?"

I stir around my beans, noting the little roasted almond slivers and freshly ground pepper mixed in. I cook a proper Thanksgiving meal each November, but it isn't half as detailed as this everyday supper. "I'm on a little break between things," I say. "We just had our graduation ceremony, so I don't need to return for a bit."

I also notice the beautiful, heavy flatware Frank owns. I've only had cheap, mismatched flatware my whole life. It's something that I'd like to correct, much like the fact that my wine glasses are mismatched, too. And I've never owned a proper, extra cushy living room recliner, and yet Frank has two. One for the dog? He also has two couches in the living room. He's into details, ones that

I've been ignoring around my house. I could afford all of this, comfortably, if I used my inheritance money. But what's the point? Whom do I have to impress? Whom does he have to impress?

"Do you ever take on any tenants, or have any long-term visitors?" I ask. "I was just noticing all of your furniture."

Franks wipes his mouth. "Well, I love entertaining. I try to do it weekly. It's just more comfortable if everyone can sit somewhere nice," he says. And again I'm envious, jealous of his ability to confidently open his home so often, when I can hardly host breakfast guests without a meltdown.

"Do you live with anyone, Mae?" he asks.

I nod. "Yes, I have a student as a tenant right now, though he graduated this past weekend, so he'll move out soon." I catch Frank smile, and feel the smile is slightly peculiar somehow.

"It's not that kind of relationship. He's really just my tenant."

Frank's smile fades. "I understand. If you've got the space, it makes sense to rent it out." Though Frank's smile was actually because Mae confirmed item one from the Captain's checklist. "See if she lives with a student," he'd told Frank. "His name is Jack, if she'll offer that much."

While Mae is smearing a dinner roll, Frank gets direct. "What's your tenant's name? What's he like?"

I set down my knife. "Jack," I say. "He's an interesting guy. Lots of hormonal stress inside of him," I tell Frank, who seems to keenly understand just what I'm saying. "Maybe you remember those days?"

And so we talk, our little friendship moving along down its road. "Are you worried about crime in Chicago?" I ask Frank. "As a homeowner?"

Frank tips his head thoughtfully. "I was when I first moved in. It's a very nice neighborhood, but in some ways that's even more dangerous because thieves see your place as a lucrative bullseye. Nothing's ever happened to me over the years, so eventually I stopped worrying. If someone wants to get in here, they're going to get in here and that's that. No sense losing sleep. What about you? Do you live in a good part of Ann Arbor?"

"I think so," I say. "Of course, Jack's been around, and that's been helpful. I'm actually more worried when I'm on vacation—worried about the places where I'm staying."

Frank looks interested. "Do you visit a lot of urban areas?"

"I do. Though actually, I suppose I was the most scared a long time ago, way up in Maine."

"Moose? Lobster?" Frank suggests playfully.

"Whales," I say. "I know, it's ridiculous. I went out on a whale watching day trip when I was younger. There's all sorts of packages you can choose from. If you want to cruise on a luxury yacht and eat gourmet food while using complimentary binoculars for spotting, you can. Or you can just take a fisherman's little motorboat out into the water with a poncho. Whatever you want and can swing, I suppose. I was on a smaller boat, but not terribly small—sort of pontoon-like in size."

Frank shifts in his chair, quite interested.

"So, we're out on the Atlantic. We'd been trolling around for over an hour and hadn't seen anything except a dead tuna fish. I was looking down over the railing when I saw bubbles surface. And then, a spray of water came shooting up. It was so close it misted my face. A moment later, a humpback crested, his bumpy body right next to the boat."

"Wow," Frank breathes.

"I know. It was completely thrilling. I knew that whales were huge. Everyone knows that whales are huge. But to see one right next to you, absolutely enormous, and much longer than the boat you're in, it's also terrifying. What was stopping him from flipping us right over? Nothing. Apparently I wasn't the only one who was scared, because a crew member said, 'Humpbacks are very friendly and curious. They like to come right up to the boats.' But for those few moments, I felt the purest form of fear. Out there in the middle of the ocean, beside a fifty-foot creature."

I've never told that story to anyone. I try not to think of it, try to quickly replace it with my items of the day, because that whale trip reminds me of my parents, and the places we've gone, and how they instilled in me the mindset that the whole country is my home; not just our house, not just my state. That it's all mine to see and care for, and that we were graced by God's generosity in our lives. I took my first airplane ride at seven weeks old, and can really say that I know where I live, that I know my home. There are photos of me asleep in a bike carrier as a baby, being towed around Portland. I recall being nudged awake in the backseat by my excited father during one trip to Missouri as he announced, "Look sweetheart, it's the Arch!" I've been to the bottom of the Grand Canyon, and the bottom of the Hoover Dam. I know the best B&Bs in the Carolinas, the nicest delis in New York, the most scenic trails in Utah. My parents showed me everything they could, constantly, like they were my life tour guides.

I've driven the deserts, all of them, all that we have here. I've seen Indian reservations, bought beautiful turquoise jewelry out in the glossy heat of Arizona from a woman with trembling hands. I've driven from California to Texas and back, wondering where narrow dirt roads go, wondering how people could survive out where the ground looks like sandstone and there's no rush of water, anywhere, for hundreds of miles. I've wondered why some people have tires on their roofs, and how others could need a dozen fancy terraces circling theirs. I've been to all of our states, and over twenty countries, all because my thoughtful parents knew that showing me how people live and what the world really looks like was the most important lesson they could teach me.

I blink away an unexpected tear as Frank and I continue talking. Dinner finishes, and Frank sets down two slices of pie before asking, "What's your religion, Mae?"

I'm taken aback. It's definitely a personal question, but really no more so than asking someone his or her political leanings, which I would take no offense to. Plus, Frank didn't ask, "Do you believe in God?"—the much more intense question that would really upset me, even if I have a sound response.

"I'm . . . not sure how to answer," I say.

Frank looks apologetic. "Didn't mean to upset you. Just thought since we were being so open, religion was alright to discuss."

But inside, Frank is tossing and turning, so hoping to get confirmation on the Captain's second area: "See if talking about religion gets to her. She's technically Catholic."

I shrug and tug at my hair, not liking this new direction. "I suppose I'm in-between religions," I finally stammer, an answer that surprises me. "From Catholic to . . . something not Catholic, perhaps. I have a problem with the Catholic Church's policy on Communion."

"Do you attend services?" Frank wants to know. "There are some really nice churches in the area if you've got extra time during your visit."

The tablecloth is now altar fabric. I feel watched, from above, from below. Is someone listening to me, too?

"I don't attend services anymore," I say truthfully. "I sometimes go to church, though."

Frank looks confused.

"I mean, sometimes I just . . . walk around the churches. I try to find inspiration."

"I'm one of those people who read inspirational quotes," Frank says, trying again to connect with her. "It's nice that someone has already done the groundwork on figuring out the human psyche. It's nice to open up a collection after dinner and do some thinking. Love those cheesy inspirational calendars, too. Have to get one every Christmas."

Me, I've never been one for inspirational quotes. "I prefer to listen to lyrics," I say, "especially bold lyrics. Ever listen to the Counting Crows? In one of his songs, Adam Duritz sings that if a guy wants to change the world, what's as easy as murder? Isn't that powerful? Doesn't that just stay with you?"

Frank looks at me for a long, long time.

I'm coming undone with a flashback of my cheerful parents leading me up a worn path in Colorado, a blue and gray sky striking against swaying golden grain. Like a painting. Like a photo. How I wish I'd taken even one photo of all of us on those many trips.

Frank is changing, I notice. His eyes look scared, his face is taut. "You know, I should go. Thank you so much for having me over. I'm glad we met," I say awkwardly.

My new friend seems suspicious now, and as a result, I'm alarmed and ready to run. I didn't confess anything. I didn't admit anything. And yet, I've given away more than a glance inside of me.

We don't exchange contact information. We don't shake hands goodbye. We merely nod, in that casual acquaintance sort of way, and I slip out the door and clip down the sidewalk. I don't turn around, but I know he's still standing on his stoop.

*

As Mae walks through Frank's Chicago neighborhood, the retired professor gestures wildly at the squad car, mouthing, *It's her, it's her, it's her* like a madman. In those last moments of dinner, it occurred to Frank, and rather plainly, that Mae was probably wanted for more than breaking into churches or shacking up with a student. They don't do regional searches for small-time criminals. And women who bring up the ease of murder at the dinner table might be a little off in the head. Mae went from being a captivating woman to an unstable woman in seconds.

The officer's car grunts to a start and the headlights snap on, illuminating the evening's bugs and pollen. The car slowly rolls down the block, just behind Mae Harrington.

*

I'm standing at the edge of Lake Michigan again. I keep coming back here. I guess I like the connection to Michigan, realizing that the other shore is my home. I'm actually standing in the very spot where I hurled Jack's gun into the water a few nights ago. It's dark, and the lake might as well be a small ocean, yet I'm convinced if I stare at the black ripples long enough, a silver revolver will pop up to the surface as easily as a bobber. The skyline is twinkling, and the city noises are present, but I feel removed and alone.

I kick off my shoes and enter the water, inhaling a slow breath before going under to search the sandy bottom.

CHAPTER
12

March 3, 1995.

The kind of sky is overhead where the clouds hang so low that tree shadows, body shadows, atmosphere shadows, are all so dark underfoot that they stain the pavement. Today the sky spilled its drink, and I'm carelessly kicking the ice cubes through the doorway of my film theory classroom. I hate the gloaming. It makes me so lonely. It's like the sun is slipping away and I can't catch it when it becomes strangled by the night. God, nothing could be lonelier.

While my pen rolls across a pad of legal paper in class, my eyes occasionally peer over the dark-headed teaching assistant to scan the clock. Once he caught my eyes as they darted up, and as my view lowered, he was definitely staring. I'm going to buy a wristwatch on my walk home this afternoon, from that little supply store that sells all kinds of junk like rubber band balls and rat poison. He probably thinks I'm just anxious to get out of here, like everyone, all of us who go home and cook our noodles, listen to cute five-dollar bands near the Santa Monica pier that we're sure will be big on the radio soon, before we go searching the night for street meat—those beautiful little tacos and burritos and pork carnitas that roll through alleys in dinged up metal carts by tipsy Mexicans. Being a college student in Los Angeles is exciting, even if this city is always transforming, perhaps ever more dangerous and dirty.

At exactly six o'clock, I bend and crack the silver foil and a white pill falls snugly into my palm. I take it without water. And as I pick up my pen to resume taking notes, I see him watching again.

He comes to me after class, and quickly. I'm packing up and ready to move, but his sneakers stop in front of my trendy brown loafers with the beads on the tassels. He drops his skateboard to the floor, but he's not going anywhere just yet.

"So do you take drugs every day at six?" the TA asks. "And which kind? Something I should try, too?"

While I'm hatching a verbal escape plan, Brian slips into the room, a styrofoam carton in his hands. He smiles warmly at me, with those little-kid eyes and baby-cheek dimples. "I brought you dinner," he tells me, setting down two giant roast beefs on rye. My TA smacks his lips.

"You mean you brought us dinner?" I ask, pointing at the two sandwiches.

"No, this is just for you. I've gotta run now—I'm singing downtown in a little while." He leans down for a tender kiss, like my instructor isn't standing a foot away, like we're the only two people around and I love it. "I love you," he whispers through my hoop earring.

"Hey," I tell him, reaching into my handbag. "Bought us a little surprise. Hope this works out with your schedule," I say, handing him an envelope with two plane tickets to Chicago on a United flight. He pockets the envelope and smiles before slipping right back out into the mud of a March in Los Angeles.

"Wow," my instructor raves, "Some people marry for less. A lot fucking less."

I give a half-smile, thinking this over.

"But is he trying to fatten you up?"

I look down at the roast beefs. "He does feed me a lot," I say, realizing that he really does bring me all sorts of food. "He likes bread. He likes to bake bread, too."

My film instructor gives a causal "huh" before getting back on his skateboard. I can hear him rattling down the hallway, and I'm alone in the room now. I didn't have to tell him that I take my birth control at the same minute, at the same moment every day, because I'm too scared to have children, ever, and can take no chances about the matter. And now that they're both gone, neither one will see me pick up all the rye bread Brian brought, give it a good smell, give each slice a little lick, then wrap up the bread and dump all the food in the trash.

I walk home through the village, which sounds cool and bohemian, but really it's just a clump of chain stores and discount places run by people who speak broken English and love the constant stream of business from students. You have to take a car to get anywhere else in L.A. from campus, so these stores have a monopoly on us. Right now, I need a watch; I need more discretion about my strict schedule.

The stores are unified by this cracking whitewash that connects them all, kind of like an open-air mall. The café where Nora and I sit is at the base of the stores. From above, I think it sort of looks like a church courtyard, but there's certainly nothing spiritual about picking up low-grade meat from the only grocery store in the area, and getting your photos from the Kodak guy who dresses in flowing white linens like we're living on some beach in Miami. The area directly around campus isn't so nice, but I don't let myself analyze it too much because this is still a neighborhood, where some families have lived for generations. Thinking too much about poverty upsets a part of me I can't fully identify or come to terms with, so I walk past the residents, books in my arms, just here as a temporary student and nothing more. It's not so much that I feel sorry for them, but that I feel scared around them. Poor people do irrational things, scary things, desperate things. They put me on the offensive.

I'm approaching the supply store when a man with a basket on his bike weaves before my feet, stopping so fast we're nearly in a heap. I back off quickly when I see his brittle teeth, cracked flour hands, jeans as filthy as a farmer's but smelling like yesterday's fast food trash from the dumpsters. "Hey!" he says, like we're long-lost lovers. "Whatchaupto, girl?"

I want to say this is a rare thing, but I feel like I'm constantly being interrupted, blocked, followed. People just start conversations with me, sometimes telling me everything, more than they tell their mothers or fathers and kids. Last week, while I was eating my lunch under an umbrella, a woman with a newspaper tucked under her arm sat down beside me and told me she's getting a blood transfusion tomorrow before she even said hello. I'm oddly approachable; perhaps it's my Midwest aura. Perhaps it's my easy face.

Today I keep my head down and pass the man. There's an issue of safety here, yes, but I've grown tired of all the forced humanity.

The man calls back to me as I duck inside the store. It'll be another twenty minutes before I get to leave with my new green flower watch because a woman in an extravagant headpiece wants to know if I have any clothes in her size that I don't wear anymore, and if not, how about some old kitchen appliances? "Well how about any food then? Anything about to spoil even?" I think about the two big roast beefs from Brian and how I threw away all that good meat and deli cheese.

"I'm leaving now," I tell her, assuring myself that the time I gave her was enough.

I'm getting plenty worked up, trying to get home with some time left in the day, avoiding eye contact and quite mad that the sidewalk is so crowded that I'm rubbing elbows with everyone and everyone is bumping along with me. I draw my purse tighter and stare at the poplar trees with their tiny buds, trying to hear the birds above the traffic, thinking about frothy ocean water, and the mountains far, far away from this city, where there isn't competition for breathing air and somewhere, a field of wildflowers is readying its display. I wish I were alone, but that's impossible in Los Angeles, where too many seeds are growing in the same sunny patch. I know that even when I'm back in my apartment, I'll hear the noises, so many noises, and think about all this rough ground around me. No wonder Brian can't sleep at night. Who the fuck can?

A traffic light flips from green to yellow, and I shove a little boy into the street, his hands smacking against the road as a Mercury Grand Marquis slams on its brakes a foot away from his head. The boy rolls onto his backpack and meets my stare, his eyes hurt and terrified, his knees bloody, his chest heaving. But my eyes are calm, my heart disgusted. He gets up and runs off between the buildings while the whole city tries to decide what to do with me. But no one says a word, lost in disbelief perhaps, not even the cop parked on the other side of the street. He must have seen everything.

I strap my new watch on while waiting for the walk sign, carefully setting the minute hand as the sun sets and a purple sky spreads west.

*

Sometimes I kiss the back of my hand. I used to do it a lot more, like when I was lonesome in college living in my little apartment between breakups with Brian, and in high school when I fantasized about kissing people, all types of people whom I hadn't met yet, and wanted to practice on something with flesh and warmth. It's a body habit, like biting your nails or grinding your teeth. I'd argue that at least it's a pleasant habit, since I'm not doing any harm. Sometimes I catch myself doing it unconsciously, which is a little disturbing, because that means other people have probably noticed me kissing the back of my hand. I was bringing my skin to my lips a moment ago when I got the shock of my life. And now, I'm standing before this shock, lips pursed in midair like a taxidermy trout.

The Chicago Symphony is playing *Mae's Turn* tomorrow, composed by Jack Mekinski. This is what the marquee tells me as I stand motionless while masses of people stream past, happy to get home after work. I lower my hand and exhale, a little water still dripping off my jeans and hair from Lake Michigan.

"Unbelievable," I whisper to myself. I was going to go straight to my hotel room to pack up and get right to sleep an hour ago. Of course I was, until realizing it was my last night in Chicago, maybe ever after this trip, and I wasn't quite done with the city. I knew I had to cross the breathy streets again, look up and notice all the quiet concrete details that make up the high squares and curves of the buildings once more. And now this.

*

While Mae is processing her thoughts, the stakeout police officer picks up his transmitter. "Interesting situation, guys," he speaks into the hand piece.

"More interesting than her evening swim?" someone responds.

"Oh yes. She just found out Jack's in town."

After a few silent moments the transmitter crackles back to life.

"What's she doing about it?"

The officer radios back. "She's in the lobby of the theater. Looks like she's waiting in line at the box office now."

*

I approach the cashier working behind the fake glass. "I'd like one ticket to tomorrow's show."

The cashier leans forward into her microphone. "Which show?"

I'm certain I'm speaking in a foreign language as I say, "*Mae's Turn.* The symphony."

The cashier touches her computer screen. "Do you have a seat preference?"

"I'll take the best available," I tell her, wondering how much this will set me back. She looks down at her screen. "Sure thing. Your name, please?"

"Mae Harrington."

"Oh! Mae Harrington. I have a ticket on hold for you."

The cashier opens a wooden drawer and pulls out an envelope. "Compliments of Jack," she says, while I stare dumbly at her face.

And with that, I recede back into the night air, plodding a familiar path to the Congress Hotel for a restless night of sleep as the city stirs beside me.

*

Jack is warming up backstage on a storage crate behind a clump of music stands. It's early Friday evening, about two hours until the curtain is drawn, and tech crews are congregating to talk about sound and lighting. When he checked in with the Captain last night, he was informed that Mae picked up the complimentary ticket. "We didn't lead her to the theater," the Captain said. "She saw the marquee on her own. A city the size of Chicago, and she still finds you." So Jack gathers that Mae is only being watched right now, which is definitely the best route. If she were being chased, who knows what she might do.

Scales float out of the clarinet, evaporating into the dense scene backstage. The Symphony loaned Jack a fine instrument, though of course playing any instrument that's not your own feels so different, so strange, like being the new guy in town walking into a bar of regulars. This one is heavier than Jack's, and the keys are a bit sticky. But it has a gorgeous, warm sound that Jack is easily falling in love with. It's so mellow, so mature.

After practicing for an hour, mostly his favorite standbys that he uses to relax his muscles, Jack breaks for dinner. He picked up a thick sandwich from the corner deli on his way over, roast beef with baby swiss. How long has Mae been in Chicago, he wonders. Did she leave right after breaking into the church? Did she see the police cars at the house? Maybe she heard news of this performance in Ann Arbor and just arrived yesterday. Jack is flustered, and would like to speak to her. But he knows he can't interfere. He's also unclear about when the police plan to make their move. Eventually, Mae will be arrested. In the meantime, she's being cornered. And Jack will watch her tonight, watch over her while he still can, since her assigned seat is rather close to the woodwinds.

As he wipes his mouth, Jack notices a copy of tonight's program sitting on a tuba case. He reaches over and scans the presentation, then allows himself to feel a little bit of awe, a little bit of pride for the first time over this whole matter. He even recognizes a few musicians' names as longtime Symphony principals, including tonight's vocal soloist.

*

I'm sitting in the concert hall. My ticket was free, and clearly this means my attendance is noticed. This may have been arranged by any number of people. I know Jack will see me. I scout the box seats high above, the ones with a clear view, uneasy and wondering who else is interested in my attendance. I came upon the theater by chance, and there was a ticket with my name on it. Wishful thinking from some law agency, perhaps? And apparently, I no longer care if I'm caught, because here I am, just missing a stage spotlight on my head.

A familiar pre-concert murmur encases the crowd of people taking their seats and adjusting their belongings. Fancy purses are gently set down, keys are making tinkly music as they transfer to pockets. The curtain is shut on stage, but it started to shift and squirm a few minutes ago. The musicians are bumping along behind the velvet, getting themselves organized and ready for their performance. I'd love to know how Mr. Confidence is feeling back there. I'm guessing our paths crossing away from home has him fairly distracted, which is too bad given this accomplishment. Seems I've ruined quite a bit for Jack lately, but there's a lot from my side he's yet to hear. And I suppose I'll have to tell him soon, if we're able to talk again.

The house lights flash, the gentle warning bells chime, and the stirring evaporates into quiet anticipation. I'm falling into a slow trance now, but I'm still aware of where I am, which is certainly where I shouldn't be. It's been an exhausting week, a reckless week, and what did I gain from it?

The musicians are presented now, an older conductor taking the podium, his gaunt and curling body still declaring a refined dignity. I can make out Jack's shape without looking directly at him, as I have seen his shape so many mornings and evenings. I sense that he is, however, looking directly at me. Strange that we're again in the same room. If he's here, who is watching over my house and feeding Oscar back in Ann Arbor?

Oh Jack, I want to ask you: did you see the last of the spring velvet leaves falling to the sidewalk outside the theater? There's still a few out there; catch them before they're pushed into the cracks by summer sandals. The food is so good in this city, full of fat and grease with international fusions; I hope you've had your fill. Tell me, did you walk the shore of my lake, did you see the art, did you watch college kids take over coffeehouses as though they were suitable offices? Did you buy a local paper, talk with a bus driver, look up and wonder how the giant spires made it to the roofs of skyscrapers? I want to show you where the street grates fill with white flower petals, blown over from Millennium Park, down where no one notices. I want to sit with you on the pier, wearing crisp blouses with simple sugar cookies in our hands; either here, or on our pier back home.

Soon Jack is bowing, and I realize that he's been introduced as the composer, though my mind and ears missed the announcement. As the music starts, as my life story is played among the cellos and violins and even a fiery little piccolo that I very much appreciate, I remember the goodness of Jack. I realize, now, that this is a gift for me. And I think about water: swimming, splashing, drowning. I think about my parents, and if their afterlife is playing out in some unusual way because of their earthly ending, and if their afterlife even exists at all. I wonder what they would think about all this, and this odd relationship I have with a student, no husband or kids in the picture. And I wonder, did they intend to give me a sibling?

I think about the differences between Chicago and Ann Arbor, and somewhere in the middle of the symphony, I allow myself to think about the concept of love and where I do and do not fit into expectations. The experience is taxing, and Jack's shape is still present just off to my left. At once, everything hurts inside me, and the strings hurt, too, and I know the symphony is getting close to its end because it's catching up to my current life, to my now, when

I'm gone.

A vocalist steps out for the last section, gingerly adjusting his lithe microphone. I don't really look at him until I hear his voice, that baritone voice that I first heard when I backed into his car in Los Angeles. His eyes look older than I remember. His face, more sunken, less familiar. He's heavier, his hair shaggy. He's really changed, and looks many years beyond his age. A thousand memories ping past me like speedy arrows. We drank smoothies for dinner when we were too busy or lazy to make something. His allergies were always worse in the fall instead of the spring. He stored laundry quarters in plastic candy containers. He had a lot of sleep issues, and bad dreams, and maybe still does.

We rented a Hitchcock film for our first date, and ended up on his roommate's bed. The windy air always flapped the curtains so strongly on the tenth story of their building, one that I'd be in and out of day and night, summer and winter, when we were on, off, together, apart. You saw a lot of L.A. darkness from that high: so many cars, so much brown and gray haze, persistent noise, always so much noise. You could tell if the freeways were moving from that high, and you could call your friends on the go to warn them. You could smell a little cigarette smoke from other tenants sitting on their fire escapes. Some mornings we cooked eggs, other mornings we took our eggs over easy in the café. Once he showed up at my gym, urgently needing to discuss the grounds for another unfolding breakup. He was always so wordy about our endings, and so sure that it was the best decision, but then, as the days passed and I went through my usual post-breakup routine, he was never really sure at all. Fundamentally, he was just a basic young person, unsure of what he wanted. And maybe I was the same, except not really, because I ultimately committed to my decisions. And now, Jack is where we were, except he's moving in the right direction, and at a much faster pace. Everyone's day-to-day story during their young twenties is a little different—some are in school, some are starting to work—but the love stories are more or less the same. And hurting hearts are always the same. That's timeless, ageless.

I remember him looking so much younger, so child-like, and now . . . he just seems so old. He is past his current age, I'm certain. Something must have happened to him.

My stomach churns. Somehow, I'm actually not surprised to see Brian. I think that these sorts of people, the ones who change you the most, can always come back to blindside you on any day—on vacation, or at your neighborhood pancake place. Our friendship circles don't overlap anymore, and our professional circles certainly don't. But the universe remembers our bond, and every once in a while, it seems a dangerous meeting is required to keep the cosmos amused, like an asteroid cruising too close to our planet and getting everyone down here all worked up.

Brian bought me a *Little Prince* calendar for Christmas one year. That's still my favorite book, my Little Prince who lives on asteroid B-612. And it infuriates me that such a precious tale is tainted because of his ten dollar bookstore buy. Tonight it seems two asteroids are causing trouble for me, as Jack and Brian, in positions I couldn't have conceived of an hour ago, are but three feet apart. Brian has no idea whom he's performing with, I'm sure, but I bet Jack knows.

The symphony ends on a loud, long finishing chord, as symphonies often do. Jack is more of a classical guy than a modern man, but I could see that changing as he explores young adulthood further. The crowd stands for an ovation. I still haven't given Jack a proper look. And I'm already busy trying to forget seeing Brian tonight, a skill I've had plenty of practice with during those up and down years in Los Angeles and beyond. As I clap, my eyes scan the box seats again, observing people's reactions. Everyone seems impressed and satisfied, except two men who look oddly out of place up there. One of the men nods at me and elbows his partner.

I don't wait for the second ovation. It's a gamble to run down the empty aisles and out the back hall door, such a dramatic and noticeable exit while everyone else is standing still, but panic sets in so that's what I do. I keep my head down, but my ears hear murmurs and ceasing applause as I run out. Once outside, I head straight northwest, hoping to reach the church I passed earlier in the week even faster by cutting through alleys and behind office buildings. Breathless and possessed, I make it to St. Peter's in just a few minutes. I don't even try the front door, instead running around to the sides. And I don't even wrap my hand as I punch out a lower window, blood mixing with glass bits on the window's frame. I slide inside, ending up on the floor right next to a row of ornate pews. I stand in the darkened church, lit only with exit signs and a slight glow from city street lamps standing guard outside. I sling my handbag over my shoulder, Jack's gun thumping against my back.

I waste no time getting to the altar. This one is rather sparse compared to others, but it's Friday night; no need to have it dressed up until Sunday. I start pulling on cupboard doors surrounding the table, but of course they're all locked. This is an urban church, and surely nothing is left to chance. I'm surprised an alarm system didn't trigger. Or maybe it did, and it's silent. Maybe I only have a few minutes in here.

And then, as surreal as anything else that's happened over the past few weeks, I see Jack's shape standing at the back of the church, just a pulsing outline.

"How did you get over here so fast?" I say. "How did you even know where I went?"

Jack walks up the center aisle, his feet remarkably silent. "This is the closest church to the hall," Jack says quietly. "I had a hunch. And I run pretty fast. I'm really fit, you know, from all those morning exercises that I do back at your house."

For a moment, we just watch our outlines, still separated by a lot of space. Then Jack gets serious. "You're going to be arrested. Soon. I can't believe you did this."

"I know. But I really haven't done anything very serious. I mean, not related to all this."

Jack tips his head quickly, face and eyes still blackened with shadows. He's like a marionette without features. "Breaking and entering into churches, at least three times counting tonight. Gun theft. Evading authorities by crossing state lines with my gun. And that's just what I know about. Somehow I bet there's more. I'd say things are at least somewhat serious, Mae."

I step down from the altar and walk up to Jack, who is now just feet away from me. I feel so strange. I reacquaint myself with his face again. He still looks young, still looks like a rebel, but he also looks like he pities me now. He's learned so much more than Brian and I did by his age.

"Maybe I am in a bit of trouble now, but I've caused trouble before. Actually, I've been in trouble for a long time, because I killed my parents."

Jack seems calm, and completely unsurprised. "No, you didn't kill your parents, Mae. I read about what happened. I've talked about what happened with investigators. I know about the accident when you were young. When you were driving in the winter, and your car went off the bridge from that damned broken plank. The ice broke. You didn't kill your parents, Mae. Is that why you're so out of control? You honestly think you killed them?"

The strangeness swirling in me is intense now. I feel defiant now. "Jack, I did in fact, absolutely, kill my parents. We were driving through the countryside. It was a beautiful winter day, cold and crisp but still sunny. The kind you like to take walks on. I had these thoughts. I kept wondering what it'd be like to see the end of someone's life. To be there when they were alive, and then, dead. To decide on death, to design a death, like they designed my childhood. You know how your mind wanders while you drive? I thought about how easy it is to actually take someone's life, and in just a few seconds, too. Do you ever think about that? Think about the restraint people show every day to not destroy someone else with a car or a gun or even their own hands?"

Jacks lips fall apart, and I hear his breathing now, soft but quickening.

"I pictured myself running the car off the road, but that'd only work if the car flipped, and we'd have to go pretty fast. It didn't seem like a sure way. They'd probably just take away my license. Maybe we'd all get hurt, too, but nothing life changing. Maybe my parents would have just temporarily lost their trust in me," I tell him.

"I remembered the bridge—the height of that bridge was significant enough to do some real damage, maybe even fatal damage. So I just convinced myself to try it, like an experiment. Just run the car right off the bridge. Just see what happens. Try to manipulate life and death. Force everything to change. I didn't think I'd die, because I knew what was about to happen and could react quickly. So I didn't worry about me. I didn't, however, plan on that girl ice skating. That still makes me sick."

Now Jack looks absolutely horrified.

"And as for my parents, well, I killed them. It wasn't a simple accident, on some slippery winter bridge. I really killed my parents, and I did so intentionally, just to see what it was like."

Solemnly, soundlessly, Jack runs his hands over his tuxedo jacket. Without a word, he points to a small microphone clipped to the outside, almost like Brian's on stage tonight. But Jack isn't going to sing any solos. A wire is dangling down the front, which attaches to a transmitter pack in his pocket. Then, Jack tugs on his ear.

Someone is listening to us. And they've heard a lot.

Like Jack, I too become silent. I don't say another word, not even as we're loaded into the back of a detective's car with me in handcuffs, or when Jack is sent inside the Congress Hotel with an officer to collect my belongings while I wait in the idling sedan with the officer's partner. Jack slides into the back seat with me again before we're taken right out of the city. He holds up the piece that I bought at the estate sale, the wonderful little cottage. "Where did you get this painting?" he wants to know. But I remain silent. I don't say a word until the next morning, in a jail cell in Michigan, when a lawyer comes to represent me.

CHAPTER 13

Captain Douglas ensures that the last of the yellow tape is rolled up at Mae's house, and that the last curious neighbor is tucked in for the night. He finds it goddamn ridiculous that his team has uncovered so little thus far and so fucking slowly, and wants to make goddamn sure that Mae isn't given a slap on the wrist and released if she's really truly fucked up and is going to start axing priests or something. Oh, what a spectacle it was emptying out the pond and diverting traffic while telling local reporters, "Nothing to see here, no further comments at this time." We'll let you know if a body pops up or anything. My God, taking an early retirement package sounds better all the time.

He kills his headlights as he approaches Nora Park. Lights aren't needed now, when his feet helped weather the piers, his hands helped plant the maples that are starting their seasonal lean into the sun. Growing up in Ann Arbor was breezy, and so wonderfully formative, which he appreciates more now that he sits in a cement building in Detroit all day. The fishermen with their dirty cracked pails will start creeping down to the water soon, no licenses in hand but protected under the smudged moonlight. When he was a boy his father would sometimes sneak him down here to do the same thing. No, lights aren't needed when this park feels like a backyard.

The pond is the centerpiece of Nora Park, about a quarter of a mile away from the main gate. Every few years the community rallies for improvements to the park, and the pond benefits the most with its stately circle of old-fashioned street lamps, its hardwood benches, and its little hot cocoa hut staffed in the winter for the ice skaters. Emptying out the pond earlier today ruffled a few feathers, and the Captain desperately wanted to say, "Hey, it's my pond, too," but that isn't professional and no one wants an emotional cuckoo running the show. But in the darkness, the pond's eerie emptiness and mushy bottom sends a chill through his childhood.

He steps down the incline, trying not to slip, trying not to crush the budding wildflowers. He stops in the soggy mud to snap on his flashlight, scanning the blankness. Obviously this area was scoured and nothing is going to pop right out while you're standing here in wet slacks in the dark, he tells himself. But still he stands, for over twenty minutes, carefully staring at each little area for signs of a disturbance.

The Captain bites his lip and shakes his head, ready to resign and approve Mae's release. As he climbs out to the pond's sandy bank with his flashlight shined on his feet, he notices deep lines between the swaying reeds. He squats for a closer look, running his finger in the grooves. "It almost looks like . . . tail marks," he says aloud, throwing a look behind him to follow the trail. "Must be from the equipment," he decides, heading back to his squad car, ready for his waiting bed.

*

I started grinding my teeth shortly after my parents died. I didn't know what was causing the pain at first and just assumed I was getting a cavity. I thought I'd have to go in for a root canal at some point, but the pain quickly escalated to dizzying levels and I realized what was going on when I started waking up during the grinding episodes. It was like being shot, in the mouth, revolver head against the teeth when the bad guy pulled the trigger. I could feel the explosion all the way down into my neck and at the top of my collarbone. I was grinding my teeth so hard I could taste tooth dust settling on my tongue like sawdust in a workshop.

My dentist was no help, and had no empathy. He wanted to fix me up with some two-grand, custom-fit mouth guard that would "last a lifetime." I told him that if I kept this up I'd need the two-grand for a budget funeral. Eventually I stopped grinding my teeth when new worries arose that weren't so serious but still required space in my brain. I just shifted the worry, really. Shifted it to my back, mostly, which carries my stress these days, with big knots that have to be rubbed out at the end of each semester. And also, I ended up in therapy.

I'm tasting tooth dust now while waiting for my release from this small cell. "Just one night in jail until your quickie hearing," an officer tells me. "Gonna process the paperwork and keep an eye on you for a bit. Make sure you're released properly." This after Jack's hidden microphone clearly captured me saying that I intentionally killed my parents. What is it going to take for people to see the truth? How do I become a believable killer? Do I need to run through campus tomorrow slashing kids with a sword or throwing homemade grenades? The judicial system is startlingly uneven, almost arbitrary.

But apparently my therapy records are substantial enough to dismiss my "claims" of murder. My therapist made it clear, and I made it clear on the audiotapes he used to record me, that it was an accident. I accidentally slid off that uneven bridge, and my parents died as a result, and of course, that would send anyone's mental health into a tailspin. Apparently I never strayed from my story of bad ice on the bumpy wood and the very frail railing we smashed through on the way down. So somehow, my admission tonight doesn't matter.

And yes, I did kill that ice skating girl, too. But that truly was an accident, a very unfortunate outcome of my decision. But no one ever brought up involuntary manslaughter. Everything is so uneven that my world is tipping over like a splashy pitcher, with everything getting totally rained on.

So I guess I'm not a murderer, just a woman whose head took a very serious turn. A woman who reinvented her past from one of bad road conditions to homicide because she can't think sanely anymore, because she has survivor's guilt. A woman who breaks into churches because her thinking is so warped she feels she needs saving from Christ and will go to any means to get it, welcomed or not. This is what the attorney tells me, who popped in for a visit an hour ago. Everyone seems to agree with his assessment, so I'm pretty sure that, yes, I'll get away with murder, one more time. Fancy that, it really happens. Right now they're probably just going to give me a community service project and charge me for the property damage done to the churches, because there's even some level of general pity for me!

Thus, if there's some actual bad news tonight, it really is the simple but brutal pain of starting to grind my teeth again. I feel that revolver head in my mouth, metal to enamel, grinding, tapping, sparking, shooting. And it makes me want to pull a trigger again. I've decided that, given my current situation, it's best to bring this up with the psychiatrist I have to see before my hearing. She stopped by tonight to introduce herself, a laptop warm and buzzy in her arms. She reviewed my rights and brought up a few things about my present, but had one pressing question that seemed to tumble from her lips before she was ready to deliver it. "Mae, do you still . . . see some people as outlines? Like they're just shapes standing in front of you?"

"No," I lied, and a few moments later, she slipped into an outline too, gray and wobbly.

Soon I'll just be resting at home, like I've taken a sabbatical. I'm still on staff at the university and everything, at least as far as I've been told. Everyone is under the impression that I'm not going to cause any further trouble if I'm stuck in my house, and at home I'm pretty much on my own. Well, that's not entirely true. In a strange turn of events, Jack's been assigned as my caretaker until the hearing. He was about to leave town, but now he's my keeper. And once again, I feel sorry for Jack. If he were my son, I'd tuck him right into bed, all twenty-two years of him, and tell him that this is just a bad dream.

I still haven't processed everything that happened in Chicago. I'm thinking about the painting I bought, and if it weren't for that physical souvenir, my time there wouldn't seem real; instead, it'd seem like a rambling woman's diary page. But I'm so responsible: an English professor, a pet and home owner. Did I really just leave Ann Arbor on foot, really make my way down to Chicago, meet Frank, see Jack, see Brian, hear my long song, leave with the police? It was dangerous. I'm so foolish. I need to put that all away, slide it back from the front of me and into a tiny backdoor memory, one that won't keep me up anymore, or create any more guilt since what's done is done. I shouldn't have left, shouldn't have gone and saw and done and now I'll always know a part of me is truly unpredictable.

One little person, but one huge problem I have reconciling, is Frank. Was I supposed to meet him? Was he yet another temporary friend, one more name on the long list of names a person creates over the course of a journey—like the guy who sells you a bagel and talks about his cousin whom, it turns out, you graduated high school with. Or like the woman at the rental car station with the same watch as you who makes you wonder what life would be like if you switched places with her. Or was Frank more? Is Frank more? Did he have something to do with my arrest? Perhaps the universe felt our meeting was necessary, for folly or purpose, just like seeing Brian and Jack together on stage in Chicago, my space asteroids on their collision course at my expense.

I feel unsettled about Frank, but I'm going to change this. I don't have to linger over strangers, don't have to keep them rolling around in my mind only to keep popping up, haunting and causing distress. Chances are, I'll never see Frank again. So why should I keep thinking about him? Obviously I have more pressing concerns. He's one more sleepless night, one more tooth lost to grinding, one more dim light to keep terribly flickering in my brain, always hoping for an adjustment.

So goodbye, Frank. Whatever we had, will remain as it was to me. May you keep doing so well.

As I'm about to lie down on my little foam bed, try to stop sorting things out for a few hours and simply rest, I see a snap of light down the corridor. I'm not worried or interested until it starts to blink-blink-blink. I see reflections, scattering, bouncing around and onto my ceiling, but I still don't hear anyone. I'm staring up at these lights when he says, "Hello, Mae."

My demon paperboy is on the other side of the bars.

I am immediately standing and frantic, trying to look down the corridors to see if anyone else is around. Aren't visitors announced?

The paperboy looks me over for a long time, too long of a time. He is motionless but intense, and I feel the last ice cubes from my splashy pitcher fall out and slide away, water spreading over eve-rything. "Did Jack send you?" I finally ask. "Is he not allowed to come?" Why else would this kid be standing here?

"Oh, I'm plenty sure that he doesn't want to come. He's over you."

As he continues to stand there, just stubbornly stand there with-out any apparent reason, I start to see hell in his heart and watch as the last angels, the ones who were holding out just in case, flap their dusty wings and head for home before the harm comes.

"So all these years of me flinging papers on your porch, and Jack never mentioned me at all? Really?" he asks.

I swallow and shake my head. "No. I take it you two are friends?"

"You don't know much about Jack's life then. Don't know how he ran off to college like some smart fuck and just left me behind, not caring what happened, obviously forgetting about me entirely if he doesn't even talk about me, didn't even explain who I was?"

I listen for Jesus, and think I might hear someone from above start to get interested, but for now, it's just me and this demon, and he's mad.

"I've never been inside a jail," I tell him, though I'm not sure why.

"You know where I've been?" he asks, leaning forward while I try to spot his tail again. "I've been in your house, today and the day before, all by myself, and you didn't even know. Try fucking knowing the people in your life. Jack's got a lot of problems now, and you're one of them."

I shudder at his admissions and ache for my quiet house again, next to the water that I haven't really gotten to know, either. I sit on the bank sometimes, watch the water's top dance and sleep, but I've never gone all the way in, never once went swimming. Sitting here, desperately hoping someone comes to haul the paperboy away from me, I wonder how life can ever really just be as straightforward again as a house by the water and my graduating tenant, my former friend, whom I forcefully pushed away.

The paperboy's back muscles tighten and he turns on his heels, leaving without saying goodbye or even finishing his thoughts. Outside, his scales drip off, blowing down the sidewalk like dandelion seeds.

*

In a memorable Chicago neighborhood, one with an air of refinement that smells like poplar trees and gladioli in bloom and varnish from decks being stained, Frank is heading out the door with his dog Sally. He cooked dinner, indulged in some bachelor chocolate pie that he picked up from the grocery store, and now it's time to do the usual circuit past familiar houses and down well-travelled streets. His little pug confidently patters along beside him, her collar jangling as they walk together as companions.

Frank rounds the corner and starts thinking about Mae again, as he always does at this intersection. Actually, he starts thinking about her on the walk over. The house where the estate sale took place, right in front of him now, went on the market as a short sale, and remarkably, even though it's a pretty haywire time in the real estate sector, it sold in a week. He wouldn't notice this house without the memory of Mae attached, but now it's become a fascinating landmark for him, the place where a lot of little things got set into motion.

He's been watching the move-in process unfold for the new owner. Several moving trucks came and left. New furniture arrived. The cable company showed up, as did a heating and cooling repairman. A hired service sprayed down the limp grass with fertilizer, the truck proudly proclaiming *Weed Man* on the side.

But until now, at this very moment with Sally rooting around in a little dirt pile, Frank hadn't actually seen the new owner. But as a middle-aged woman named Delphine with soft curly hair steps out onto her stoop just as Frank looks up, he knows an introduction is coming.

One year later, the house will be for sale again, when Delphine moves in with her new husband Frank and his pug Sally.

CHAPTER 14

Brian Reynvik stands at his kitchen counter in downtown Chicago. Small cooking dishes surround him like flower petals, each filled with ingredients for his specialty bread: yeast, flour, oats, honey, and a few things he keeps quiet about. It's very late, and he should be in bed, but rather than risk another nightmare about the ice skater who's been haunting him since college, he's out here being productive.

He started making bread when he was a teenager. His wife Delores thinks it's so sweet and romantic the way Brian bakes fresh loaves of bread all the time for dinner, and for gifts, and sometimes just to have a nice aroma in the morning while everyone is getting ready for their day. When they go to a party and Brian waltzes in with "I made this just for you—I hope you like it," everyone melts into "Oh, Brian, you're the best!" He's crafty and good in the kitchen, they think. He's talented all-around, obviously. He's got a streak of old-fashioned charm, they conclude. And oh, that voice.

It's a nice cover. Not that making bread isn't a good and delicious hobby. But the research says certain doughs make the better remedy, so those are the ones that he makes the most often. Delores knows his "favorites," but doesn't suspect anything more. It's so outrageous, who would?

Brian reaches under the kitchen island for his heaviest bread pans. He likes to break out his better cookware after a successful night of singing. He used to store all of his pots and pans on top of his cupboards until he experienced an earthquake in California. It's not good to store your heaviest items above you when you're on a fault line. After a mere 4.5, a chili pot tumbled down and smashed his computer monitor. In the Midwest, storing things above you is a great space saver, but on the west coast, you've got to keep things at eye level. The first time he felt a quake out in L.A., his instincts told him to run outside, and so he did. He grabbed his girlfriend Mae's hand and pulled her with him, wobbling and veering sideways out the door. "This isn't a fire!" she yelled. "We're supposed to be in a doorframe!" But instincts are hard to ignore.

He takes out a waxy sheet of dough from the fridge, created yesterday morning when Delores went to work early. He presses it into the backs of his hands. Brian isn't making dough balls tonight for a fresh loaf to eat; he's doing his secret treatment. He starts working the meaty dough into his knuckles, smoothing it down to his wrists. Crusty Italian works well, but so does the Light Rye. He'll have to add all of this to his notebook later, where years of cryptic comments about yeast proportions and supply stores are kept for further study in his bedside drawer, always within arm's reach.

His mind drifts during the repetitive work. A Chicago spring is blowing through his open kitchen window in puffs, smelling of tourists with their cologne and plastic shopping bags, and marathon runners too, and an occasional dewy scent that's mixed with a little garbage and hot roof shingles. It's just all over everything, outside and in. Over everything, a mindset that he relates to lately. Over working late on stage, over early rehearsals, over his moody wife, over his . . .

Feet patter down the hallway and into the light; small feet, with stubby toes. Six-years-old now, but still with a little newborn in his eyes. Those first few hours in the hospital return to Brian often. His son's wrinkled, wet skin in his hands. A blank mind, no awareness of pain as a concept, no self-identity to screw up and screw over. "Come here, Josh," his father instructs. "Did you have a bad dream?"

"No, I'm thirsty."

Dad nods toward the fridge. "You can take a glass to your room. Don't spill."

Brian watches Josh leave, his young pale skin absolutely radiant under the warm kitchen lights. Brian finishes at the counter. The phone rings.

Picking up the receiver is tricky, but he's not going to waste the dough. This batch is particularly dense, and forms so well to his hands.

"Hello, this is Brian," he says.

"Hi, Brian, this is Captain Douglas from the Detroit police station. If you've got a few minutes, I need to ask you some more questions about Mae."

Brian is instantly irritated. "But I answered all of your questions last time."

"You did. Then you also called Mae to let her know about our chat. But as far as I know, you didn't tell her anything. Is that right?"

Brian's hands twitch under the dough. When he was with Mae, they had something very intense, something one doesn't forget. The guilt lingers a bit, too, especially when he walks along the Lake Michigan shoreline. She loved the shore. He left her stranded. But young love is transitory, and he was unstable. There's never a guarantee in relationships. Never an even 50-50 split of love, even if you're married. Someone always feels a little more, and the other, a little less. You can dance at your twenty-fifth wedding anniversary, surrounded by gifts and cake and pricey champagne, with guests who drove in, and guests who flew in. There are kids, and timeshares in the Caribbean, and beloved traditions like annual fall carriage rides under the golden elm leaves, but always, someone a little more, and someone a little less.

"Anyway, Mae's been arrested, the details of which I can't divulge," the Captain says. "She may stand trial at a later date and would need character witnesses. We're particularly interested in character witnesses who knew Mae in her teen and college years. Seems you fit the bill. Would you be willing to testify under oath?"

Brain swallows. "Testify to what? What are the charges?"

"I can't discuss the exact nature right now, sir. We're still gathering evidence and—"

"Why do you want character witnesses from so long ago? Did she do something back when we were in school together?"

"Mr. Reynvik, again, this case is ongoing. There may not even be a trial. Either way, I need to know if you're willing to testify if need be. Gotta get moving on this paperwork. And I'd appreciate it if you don't speak to her."

Brian touches the corners of his eyes, webbed with grooved wrinkles, like he squinted too hard for too long. "Yes, I'll cooperate."

"Good," the Captain replies. "Also, just so I can pass on some information to her lawyer, did she ever mention her parents to you?"

"It's been forever since we talked, you know?" Brian says exasperated. "She probably did. Who doesn't talk about their parents?"

"Well, you'd probably know if she did, because they died before you two met."

Brain inhales sharply, Mae's face back in his hands. "Oh, I wasn't aware of that. No, she didn't tell me."

*

Her feet flatten the long weeds as she walks, a basket slung over one arm. Pam is picking berries today, nature's free dessert right outside her door. She spends a lot of time in this field, and knows that Jack and Jeremy did as boys. Jeremy still spends a lot of time out here, probably getting high. There aren't any hiding places in her small trailer, no place to be unseen while doing dirty deeds, something Pam knows well as she edges closer to the woods.

The markings on the rock are fading now, but Pam can still make out her art. If anyone wandered out this way, they'd just see it as designs—almost pretty, in fact. But there was a time, when Pam was young, probably Jeremy's age, when those markings were burned into the rock with purified oils. It was the Eye of Ra pagan symbol, and still sort of is if you know what to look for. Pam used to believe in witches and fairies before she believed in Christ, not only because it was trendy but because it was more fun. On a grainy autumn afternoon, without her parents' permission, she even rode a bus down to Chicago for a hush-hush occult meeting, where she felt empowered and inspired for the first time in her life. As the group threw braided offerings into Lake Michigan, Pam laughed the laugh of someone stunted but changing inside.

But even though she's asked Christ for forgiveness in the past, she knows she can't be forgiven. And so, she is changing again. A lousy husband, now invisible somewhere in the Dakotas but apparently making great money, and two reckless sons have a way of really warping a mother, of making her do bad things. Fingering her cross necklace, she says her common little prayer. "It's time to hurt Jack. It's time to teach that ungrateful kid a lesson. Let's do this together."

*

Jack packs his belongings inside Mae's house. One way or another, easy or hard, with or without Mae's approval, he's definitely moving out. Chicago seems promising, so he might as well start there. The day after the symphony, he was offered a respectable paid internship. All things considered, that's a great gig. He also spent the day after the symphony working with cops to ensure that, yes, he'll temporarily keep an eye on Mae and will alert authorities immediately if she disappears again so they can keep the overcrowded jails a little less crowded until her punishment rolls around. Not that he feels great about this. Not that he needs any good citizen stars, either.

He's talked to Mae a few times since they've been home, but only about necessary tasks. You have a stack of bills on the counter. The vet called about the cat's annual exam. Your gutter cleaning guys want to know if they should come clean or not. Mae is a shadow of what she was. And this is the way he's going to leave her, now no more attractive to him than a polluted sea.

As the day wears on, Jack finally tells her, "I'll be gone by the end of the week. Renting a little studio in Chicago. I'm not sure what this means for you. Maybe you'll have to wear one of those ankle bracelets. Maybe worse. I don't know. Call someone about it so I don't get fucked in the process."

Mae stays silent.

As Jack heads into the living room to pack books, there's a familiar thump at the screen door. He quickly changes direction and steps out onto the porch.

"Jeremy," he calls. "Can I get that key back?"

The paperboy looks up under his dirty baseball cap, his copper eyes nearly identical to Jack's. "I left it at Mom's," he says, standing in the middle of the front walk. "Do you need it tonight?"

"In the next few days," Jack says, looking at his younger brother with a little more interest than usual, knowing he won't be seeing him much anymore. "Tell Mom hello for me, and that I'd like to see her before I move. I really would. I could stop by."

"You're moving?" Jeremy asks. "Are you at least going to give us your phone number, or are you gone for good?"

Jack swallows. "I know I've been a dick to you, Jeremy."

"You've hurt Mom a lot worse."

Jeremy's eyes shift to the side of Jack, narrowing as Mae glides onto her old porch like a filmy ghost, her hands reaching for the worn rails. "You two are brothers?" she asks.

"Is your crazy girlfriend going with you?" the paperboy remarks before getting on his bike again, delivery bag slung over his shoulder.

*

An hour later, I find Jack out on the pier, a nail hanging out of his mouth. He reaches to his side for a tape measure and murmurs something like, "Still not level, Christ."

I sit on the edge of my lawn, watching him work until he notices me. He sits back on his knees when our eyes meet.

"What now?" is all he offers.

"Finally got around to the pier, I see. Thanks for coming back to it."

"Yeah, well, I don't like leaving unfinished business."

"Our paperboy is your brother? Is our mail lady your sister?"

Jack looks down at his hands. "Mae, this is really complicated. My family situation, it's not good. I don't like to talk about it."

"That's fine, Jack. You don't have to talk about it. But please understand my shock here."

"I don't find it all that shocking. Weird, maybe. Not shocking."

You would if I told you why. You would if you knew that your brother occasionally appears to me with a tail, and that, oh yeah, he even appeared in front of my jail cell, just materialized before me to talk about you. But we've never been fully honest with each other, so why start now.

Silence widens. It's such a lovely afternoon, basically early summer now, gently warm and still, the water so inviting and at peace. "It's interesting that I don't know a lot about you, even after living with you for years," I finally say, listening to Jeremy's reasoning in my head. "Tell me, what's the worst thing you've ever done?" I'm not sure why I say this. Perhaps for one last bit of closeness, of confession. And after this Jeremy business, I feel like Jack's hiding something.

Jack clears his throat. "I don't want to go down this path with you, Mae. I just want to finish my work out here and maybe make some lemonade. Maybe some hard lemonade. Maybe take a walk down to the park by myself, get another view for a while."

But I'm persistent, intensely eager for an answer, almost rowdy for one. "Come on. You're leaving in a few days. What if we never see each other again?"

Jack looks at me, and I know he's going to let me win, like he always does.

"Alright fine, but if you don't like what you're going to hear, you've only got yourself to blame."

A blissful win.

"Turns out we're not all that different, you and me, Mae, because I've done some breaking and entering myself. Should I continue? This is brutal stuff."

"Yes," I say, not so happy anymore. Now I think I'm the one with the tail.

"My best friend was a guy named Stephen. We were inseparable from elementary school through high school. I was crushed that he chose to go off to Arizona for school, but that's what people do; they go away for school. But we made a pact that summer before college. We both had a lot of problems with our mothers, so we promised that if either of us died young we had to mom-proof for each other."

Jack waits awhile before continuing, his neck muscles tensing and releasing.

"Well, Stephen died in a car accident at three in the morning. He was drunk. I was notified around five, and by nine I was on a plane to Phoenix. Stephen's apartment was locked, so I took off my sweatshirt, wrapping it around my fist as I shivered topless, even in the Arizona heat. I was so scared, so profoundly hurt and delirious. The glass cut my back as I slid in through the window I punched out. I put on his jacket from the coat rack to soak up the blood. Then I got worried about someone calling the police, like another tenant, or his family coming along and calling the police after finding a scene like that, so I had to do a lot of sloppy cleaning up along the way. God, it was all such a mess. Such a painful, terrible mess."

Jack waits longer before going on this time. I can tell he's really hurting. I shouldn't have done this. I keep putting Jack through so much, and I really don't need to hear this story.

"I went to Stephen's room first. I cleaned up all of the *Playboys*, dragging the big box into the hallway. I went through all of his photo albums and picture shoeboxes, tearing up evidence of boozy nights and crazy women. Those went into garbage bags."

This is irresponsible of me and totally unnecessary. And yet, I don't interrupt him.

"I found pot in his desk. I had no idea Stephen smoked pot. But there are things you only learn about someone after they die. The pot went into a garbage bag too, as did some strange leather straps.

I couldn't tell if the straps were sex toys or what, but I wasn't going to take any chances. Then came the hard part. I had to turn on his computer and go through his files. But it was taking so long, and I knew someone would come to his apartment eventually. Certainly his family was going to show up and start the horrible process of grieving and trying to figure out what to do."

Jack's voice shakes. "Was I supposed to delete his checking account information? Was I supposed to delete his poetry? There were photos of people I didn't know. There were new emails waiting in his Inbox that he didn't see, emails he received after he died. Was I supposed to read them? Hell, was I supposed to *respond* to them? I was at that desk for over an hour, every second terrified that the police or his family would find me. Finally my anxiety escalated too high. So I filled the bathtub with water and threw his computer right in. It sizzled, it sparked. It was a stupid thing to do, but at least the damage was irreparable. I toweled the computer off and put it back in his office. Also a stupid thing to do, since I set up a potential electrocution. I was paranoid for a full year after that, worried that someone would realize I fucked up that computer. But nothing ever happened. I don't know how things unfolded out there. He had a funeral back here. It was . . . strange. Unnerving."

Jack's crying now. "But, I did my job. I kept my promise. I got all of his sins out of the way before his parents arrived. Of course, he died drunk, but if that's all his mother really knows, she's a lot better off, because some of those photos were just awful. Perhaps she packaged it up as a one-time mistake. I've never stopped thinking about Stephen, or that morning, and I know I never will. And now I'll be thinking about you, as I walk the streets in the city that affected you, in the city that arrested you."

It's all too much and I grab Jack, holding him around his

shoulders as he cries. Eventually he turns his face to me and we stay forehead to forehead for a long, long time as the sky tints pink, orange, gray, navy. His tears taste like cucumbers as they fall on my mouth, and my focus creeps down the pier. I wonder if I'll picnic with another.

CHAPTER 15

It's night now. The cat is curled up on my braided hallway rug. The house tucked herself in for the night, but the humans are still stomping around like rude house guests. Jack finally finished the pier, in the dark, while I sat and picked grass on the bank, drizzling little green bits over my bare legs. We ate squash risotto afterward and drank all the cabernet in the house by eleven, a shared good-bye present. Now we are a miserable lot, accomplished but woozy.

"I wish I were older," I say, surprising myself and confusing Jack.

"Older? What woman wishes that?"

I'm sitting on the floor of Jack's bedroom, watching as he sorts odds and ends in his closet.

"Well, I keep thinking that if I were older, I'd be stable. I'd be more mature. I wouldn't react with such . . . simplicity. Such quickness. I'd think things through. I'd be slower. I'd be more careful, because biologically, I'd just be slower. And all of this current drama would be over. Presumably."

"Definitely. I bet you'll be in much better mental shape when you're older. So hang on to your figure," he says.

Jack tosses a binder into a box. His face looks so worn. I think he's lost a little weight, too.

"You're so melancholy and crass now, Jack. You've lost your

fun youthful pop. Is it my fault?"

He doesn't stop sorting.

"Do you have any regrets, Jack? Did you get what you came for in college?"

Jack exhales noisily, clearly tired. "I used to love talking with you, Mae. It's hard now. I just want to get out of here. I'm sorry." He opens another binder, shakes his head oddly, and throws it in the trash.

"I'm sorry for everything, Jack. Just everything. I really am. For the rest of my life, I'll think about what I should have done differently. I'm sure you would have preferred the dorms, or a fraternity. Anything but this," I tell him.

"We're just roommates for a few days—polite, respectful roommates, I hope. I don't know why you like these episodes so much," he says.

"Just talk to me once more. Please."

And he does.

"I wanted to screw a lot of girls, fall in love my last semester, plan a little wedding. Then buy a small house that I could work on during the weekends when I wasn't playing in concerts. If you look at my time in college from a bit of an angle, with a bit of a squint, some of this happened," he begins.

"I also wanted to forget my family, wholly and totally, because of the anguish they cause me. I have clear memories of telling my mother, 'I didn't ask to be born,' and no seven-year-old should have to say that. But to my family, I was nothing but a burden. Not a son, not a brother, a burden, even though I kept out of everyone's way by holing up in my room listening to music and I really don't fucking understand why I was the reason for any of their problems when I was so purposefully invisible. The only explanation I have is that my parents weren't ready to have me and resented the cost and stress I put on their marriage with my existence. Funny though, because my brother, my shithead brother who delivers newspapers, was often seen as a precious fucking kitten. So did Mom just rally and finally get her act together for him? I don't fucking know. I don't know how things are between them now, because I don't visit her. I don't know what she's up to. Maybe she really hates him now that he's older. None of this should matter to me anymore, but it does. It just doesn't make any fucking sense, and so I can't let it go."

I look down at my hardwood floors, studying the grain lines. This floor was installed before I moved in, before I was born. I always thought this house would be great for a growing family. The floor probably held young feet, running fast to get outside and down to the river. There's a small water stain near the hallway steps. I've always pictured a little girl standing there in her '50s swimsuit, the suit fuzzy on the bottom from her sitting on the splintered pier. She waited on that stain for her towel, waited for her drying-hug.

"Family always matters, Jack. Especially families that are strained, that are unhealthy. You can't just . . . pretend or forget. You'll always try to process your youth. And if you end up having kids, you'll overanalyze their youth, too, each day, even while they're busy living it."

"Do I have any regrets about college, specifically?" Jack says, seemingly ignoring my transition. "A few months ago, I would have said that I'm not going anywhere until I have my way with you. Until I make you, gently or forcefully, finally find me attractive, but you just never did. I also regret that I'm only now getting emotionally invested in your mental health, as our little life together blows up, because I could have prevented this cerebral catastrophe. I like happy endings, but neither of us got one for this

time period. Crazy: you want to be older, and I'm terrified of growing up."

"Oh, I think you have grown up. A lot. Really, Jack."

Jack bites his lip and shakes his head. "Not really, Mae. I kept a
gun in my drawer just in case my mother showed up. That's how
much I want to avoid her. I'm still so young. I'm just so young."

I feel sick again, as I so often do these days.

"You'd kill her, Jack?"

Jack looks surprised, then falls sullen. "No, Mae. I'm not you.
I'd kill myself, not my mother."

"Mine weren't bad parents," I say, thinking about my own mom.

"No?" Jack asks.

"Not at all," I say.

"And yet you say you killed them anyway? They didn't threaten
you or make you feel completely unwanted? They didn't abandon
you? They just crafted you into a good, well-rounded kid? How
terrible. How unspeakable."

"It really wasn't about them. It was about me. I was in this . . .
mood. This particular state of mind. I just wanted to see what
would happen. I think people fantasize about murder all the time.
Someone cuts you off on the highway, and you pull up beside
them with a pistol drawn. Wouldn't it be sweetly pleasurable to see
their reaction, to make them fear you? Wouldn't it feel intensely
powerful to be so unpredictable? But I was crazy then. I still am. I
recognize this. I don't trust myself."

"So you're less of a murderer and more of a reactionist?" asks
Jack.

"Maybe."

"Have you ever wanted to kill me, Mae? You know, for being a
young flip kid? For treating girls like shit? Just whip out a pistol,
professor, to teach me a lesson? Watch me get scared of you, and

you'd love that, and then just blow me away?"

"Are you kidding?" I ask at a whisper.

"No."

"I haven't. Not once," I state. "You've always done more harm to yourself than to me. You've got to watch out for you."

*

Jeremy is walking through the hay field by his mother's trailer. There's the usual mix of insects and animals this time of day: crickets, frogs, and the piercing drone of some brown beetle Jeremy calls "the annoying fuckers." They keep him up at night, his broken window propped open with an old phone book. When he was a kid, his mother released his cat in this field, unable to feed it anymore and hoping it'd just find a home among the weeds and mice. Every once in a while, though twelve years have passed, Jeremy listens for his old cat, just in case.

It's a small trailer court, consisting of one ring road around the outside and an interior road that dead-ends into a patch of green space by the mailboxes. Most of the trailers are total shit piles, but a few owners have made their tiny lots into little estates. The Bakers have a corner lot that backs up to one side of the woods, and they've done a nice job with landscaping, and added a tasteful Northwoods theme so that it almost looks like a cabin instead of a trailer. The woods are definitely the best feature of the trailer court, surrounding it on all sides except for the open field area. There's even a path in the woods that leads down to a gorgeous river. The path is marked *Private Property*, but no one is sure who owns it and all the residents certainly use it. There's another path that winds down to a campground around the same river. Without the woods, this would all be an exposed shit pile. But with the woods, so stately and almost fantasy-like in their depth, it's at least a private, nicely accented shit pile.

Jeremy's mom inherited her trailer from her mother. Based on the amount of rust and rotted-out stumps that decorate the area, this trailer court is pre-WWII. Perhaps there are some original, first-ever residential trailers sitting here. Perhaps some of them would have been worth something, had anyone cared enough to preserve them.

He watches his mother stand in the distance, near the front of her flower patch. She dusts off her jeans and heads inside. The day is slipping away now, the hot sun level with his eyes. He used to dread his mother's evening conversations, when she's always particularly tired and moody, but after this many years, it's all just more of the same now. Time to go inside and begin the ritual.

"Did you see your brother or that whore he lives with today?" she wants to know as soon as Jeremy's inside, standing on the thin plastic carpet that covers most of the floor. A lot of people consider this "outdoor carpet," but it's a pretty standard flooring choice around here, especially after the initial cheap fabric carpet wears away. This fake stuff is so durable.

"Yeah, he wants the key back. He's moving soon."

Pam's nostrils snort wide. "Excuse me? Where the fuck is he moving to?"

"I don't know. You didn't send him a graduation card, did you?"

"Why the fuck would I do that after he uninvited me?" Pam pulls at her hair, gray and feathery near the roots. Her hair is dry year-round now, not just in the winter. She's read a change in diet can help, but rubbing a raw egg onto her head every once in a while seems moisturizing enough. Just like a fancy day spa.

"I suppose you're going to leave me soon too, huh kid?"

"Haven't left yet, Ma," Jeremy says before disappearing into his room; the only room he's ever had.

*

In a cramped doctor's office in Chicago, Brian fills out a new medical history form. He has to fill these out pretty often because he switches doctors pretty often. Doctors bring him down. They're always looking for something to fix, but don't take his problem seriously because it's not something terminal, or something dangerous, like bad asthma, or even something basic and treatable. There just isn't enough to work with here. His blood pressure is wonderful. He's never had any surgeries. His bones are strong. His cholesterol is perfect. He's on track healthwise, all the professionals tell him. But today at the dermatologist, he's going to make his case otherwise.

A short woman with a pudgy frame enters the room. Her clothes are tight and bunching. She's quite happy. She has cute statement shoes and red eyeglasses. "Good morning, my name is Dr. Henderson. Looks like you're a new patient at this clinic, correct?"

"Yes. I haven't had much success in other clinics," Brian tells her.

"I'm sorry to hear that. What brings you in today?"

"I'm older than I should be," Brian states.

She chuckles. "So you're seeing some lines and wrinkles you're not liking. That sort of thing?"

Brian shakes his head. "No, not really 'that sort of thing.' I have lines and wrinkles. So many lines and wrinkles," Brian says, clutching his ugly worn hands. "Too many for my real age."

The happy doctor's smile fades. "Your real age?" she questions.

"I'm not really thirty-seven. I'm only nineteen."

Dr. Henderson shifts in her chair. She hasn't taken any notes yet.

"You're not trying to crack a joke, right?" she asks, confused but also feeling a little bit of panic. She's seen a lot of crazy patients lately. Unusual for summer. Much more common during the long

Chicago winters.

"No, I'm not cracking a joke. I know for a fact that I'm only nineteen."

"And how do you know this?"

"A young man with a tail comes to me in dreams. He keeps telling me about my childhood, and how my real age was frozen when some ice skater died in the water. Our souls started transferring to one another, me and the ice skater, but something went wrong. I can never figure it all out because the dreams are terrifying, with this car crashing through a bridge railing while I seem to sit in the back seat, and I just try so hard to wake up fast and get out of there. But I know for certain that I'm only nineteen."

Now Dr. Henderson writes notes: "Refer to Mental Health. Order general lab work-up." She looks at her new patient, carefully trying to assess his condition, really trying to imagine his world. "Well, my area of specialty isn't dreams, I suppose. Is there anything I can help you with regarding your skin? Collagen injections for better elasticity, perhaps? A prescription moisturizer?"

Brian stands and leaves, slamming the office door behind him. "Never again," he shouts, his rich baritone voice ringing off the walls.

He thinks of many important matters and considerations on his way to O'Hare. He completes a full review of his responsibilities. And yet, while a few compelling people are worth sticking around for (namely his son), he decides to deal with whatever becomes of his actions another time. They'll probably track him down in a day or so, seeing as this isn't days of yore where one could just hop on a horse and disappear into the snowy mountains. But disappearing on an island in the middle of the Pacific sounds equally enchanting, if also completely reckless and selfish, too. It's something a teenager would do, he thinks, justifying his purchase at the ticket counter.

"One ticket to Fiji," Brian states happily.

CHAPTER 16

In my house, on an early Ann Arbor evening, I hear the clarinet whale once more. My ocean, it's so different now: it's Jack's leaving, and me left behind. I've started thinking more about Heaven and Hell lately. I probably won't go to Heaven, but if I did, I think there'd be this shifting, evaporating timeline. I'd be there, but back here in Ann Arbor, Jack would be arranging and attending my surely small funeral, and boxing up and selling my possessions, and trying to decide what to do with the house; seeing as I have no family, I know he'd take on the responsibility. All of this would take place over the course of weeks, maybe months, while I just sort of stood in the general vicinity of Heaven, taking a look around. Something tells me this idea might be close to Purgatory for borderline cases like me. But maybe my Maker doesn't find me so borderline.

I hear low clarinet notes diminish to nothing, then hear the recliner's footrest click into place. In a moment, Jack is with me again. In some ways, it feels like he's always been with me. Like we've been living with each other for as long as we've both been kicking around thoughts, taking up space, ambling on through this world.

"Hey, who has your gun?" I want to know. "It's not just roaming around out there, is it?"

"I presume it's down at the police station. But it could be roaming around, maybe with the bad guys. That's what the pro-gun nuts always say; the criminals, they'll get their guns anyway, so let everyone have one. Bang, bang, bang."

I purse my lips together. I can feel permanent frown lines forming under the pressure. Good, I think. One step closer to old.

"Well, I want you to call and make sure," I tell him. "I don't want you leaving and me wondering."

Jack puts his hands in his pockets and nods agreeably. "That's fine. If it makes you happy, Mae. There's one thing I want from you, too, before I go down to Chicago."

"What's that?"

"I'm leaving in the morning. I want you to come home with me tonight."

My lines snap open into an awkward hold, my mouth agape. "I'm confused."

"Not this home. My childhood home. I want to say goodbye to my mother and Jeremy. I don't really want to do it alone. I think it's going to be really fucking ugly."

"Like dangerous?"

Jack seems amused. "No, not dangerous. I don't think either of those totally unmotivated people is capable of much more than yelling and being filthy. I just think it'll be a head trip. Probably a massive guilt trip, too."

There is a quiet sadness in his last sentence. "But you know I'm not supposed to leave the house," I tell him.

"And who will tell on you?"

I rub the pale window blinds with my fingers before answering, "Yes, I'll go with you. Wanna just go right now and get it over with?"

His eyes meet mine, and a familiar sense of belonging stitches the air closed between us. "Yeah. Let's just go now."

Jack's shape is weak and narrow as he walks out my front door, our front door. He pulls a tiny bud off a shrub as he goes, tossing it into the air like parade confetti. He's alone now. I feel it.

I sit in the passenger seat of my car. Jack won't let me drive since I "zone out and get fucked up," but I suppose when he leaves tomorrow I'll have to take up the job again, if I'm legally permitted to do so. My quickie hearing didn't tell me anything.

We head down a standard two-lane highway west of town. I don't get out this way much, but somehow it feels familiar. I guess it's just because a lot of rural Michigan looks the same. There's lots of space between houses; mostly just fields with long irrigation sprayers. Sometimes a utility cluster is quietly buzzing, or there's a car for sale in someone's yard. After a few minutes, Jack slows the car and puts on the signal.

A tiny sign is poking out of the woods proclaiming *Riverview Estates*. A long unpaved driveway of sorts eventually opens up into a small and painfully old trailer park. "One can really use 'estates' quite liberally," I remark. I turn to Jack, who has a gray hue under his paleness. He is, most certainly, feeling as sick as I have lately.

"I hate being here," he says from his little place far away. "I hate having to do this."

Meanwhile, I'm a bit excited about being here. It'll be nice to have a glimpse into Jack's past, to see where this cocky kid came from, to imagine Jack as a rough and tumble boy with dirty fingernails and frayed jeans.

A young girl rides by on her bike, an orange sucker making her lips bloated. She pulls into a grass clump and wiggles excitedly over nothing, as kids often do. As she turns to us, I see her thin legs already have some mosquito bites, and her arms are already getting tan.

"This is where you grew up, right?" I ask. He nods and slows the car to a crawl. "Right in that very trailer."

And just like that, I feel scared about our meeting.

Jack turns off the car. "I didn't realize how poor my mom is until just now," he confesses. "I was one of those poor kids, those leechy poor kids who are dependent on everyone else and have shitty moms," he continues. "I was the stereotype. In a trailer, no less."

Poverty scares me. The desperation of poor people really scares me, the way they're always on you for money, food, a conversation, something, anything. I remember this; I remember inner-city Los Angeles and those vagrant people suffocating me around campus. But instead I tell him, "You had nothing to compare yourself to as a kid. The very idea of being in poverty probably never crossed your mind. Look at that girl on her bike," I say.

The girl seems to hear us, looking over with soft and interested eyes. I remember pushing that boy into the street back in college. He was probably the same age.

I exhale and continue. "To her, life is just suckers, and trees to look at. She's got space to play in and a smile on her face. I bet she's happy. She doesn't know any other life."

"Maybe," Jack says. "Maybe. I mean this kind of poor, this is backwoods Midwest poor, you know? I'm not saying I stayed up at night listening for gunshots. I never had to hide in my closet or put a pillow over my ears. This isn't Chicago poor. No one shoots each other here. But I certainly wasn't happy. It wasn't suckers and trees for me."

Jack opens the car door. I follow him, doing my best to detach, to just be an actor in a play. Except that as I walk up the porch steps, I decide this isn't enough, and say a quick prayer, too.

What was my childhood like, anyway? Why do I have so much

trouble remembering? Praying gets me thinking about those hot roast beefs from church again. Sometimes I rode to Sunday School in the back of the truck; my father would drive extra slow and I'd hold on to the sides or the wheel wells. I'm sure that sort of thing is illegal now, if it wasn't back then.

I bet there's a lady or two in this trailer park who cooks up hot roast beefs in her slow cooker, setting the timer to ding around the end of church. This seems like a slow cooker kind of place. That's about all it has going for it.

I pray harder.

"Are you praying?"

My attention returns to Jack and standing on this stoop, like some kind of awkward date, waiting to be introduced to his mother.

"I was, yes."

"It's about time," he says, sounding relieved. As he reaches to knock, the door rips open and an angry face looks me up and down.

"Well, I know I didn't invite you two over for dinner, so what the hell are you doing here?" Jack's mother wants to know.

I see her face, damaged and unforgiving, and I start to remember. My mother used to make us all sorts of food. She didn't have to work, because my father made a good living as a corporate manager, so she spent a lot of time perfecting dishes. She went on this worldly kick for a month, and we had plates and bowls and trays inspired from Asia and Africa and the Caribbean. She printed out little country flags to stick in each meal with toothpicks.

My mother didn't have to do anything. She could have just lounged in a chair in the backyard in a cute dress with a cocktail, sort of glamorous and expensive, like a fancy mother from a lost era. But she spent each day making things easier for us. I think she

could have afforded hired help too, but she wanted to do everything herself, for us, because she saw that as her purpose. I never
did laundry, never packed my lunch. Never had to worry about a
ride, never worried about having the clothes I wanted or the books
I craved. Never worried about anything, really. She even took care
of my pet, the one that was supposed to teach me responsibility.

"Your father would be so disgusted by you, shacking up with
some older whore. You're just a kid, Jack! I hope you didn't fucking knock her up!"

Where is Jack's dad, I wonder? I have a feeling that Jack wonders
this, too. I'm scanning our many conversations now, nicely filed
and sorted for when I need to wonder about something during a
walk, or at a checkout line, or here on this sagging porch in this
uncomfortable trailer park that I'll constantly think about now.
Jack only loosely relayed that he didn't get along with his mother.
I could tell that they weren't close, at all, but I didn't imagine this
sort of tension, this kind of hate. I don't think he's ever really mentioned his father . . . oh, except that time in the store when we
were buying the antenna. He said he got money from his father.
I'm trying to assemble what all of this means, but Jack's mother
grows too frightening to ignore.

She is a bull, a python, a wolf, something not all herself anymore,
her face contorting and changing with the ease of a schoolchild's
putty. The attack keeps coming, so many words and horrors, humiliating her son, her talented, maturing, and remarkable son, who
is standing here hoping for a simple goodbye. I know he'll never
come back, never see her again. This is it, and he knows it, too.

Jack never yells back, just stands there, eyes glassy, arms stiff and
motionless. I can't even read his face, as it's so blank and distant
that surely he's blocking all of this out. He's gone now, my clarinet
whale, gliding ever deeper into the sea.

Pam's voice is getting louder, but everything is starting to sound quieter in my mind. Soon it's like I've fallen asleep with the television on, her voice now muted and removed. My gaze falls back down the porch steps, and over to her flower garden near the road.

I see him, my paperboy. Jack's brother Jeremy is standing in the garden, watching the three of us with black eyes. He rocks back and forth, and I see it again, his tail, gently swooshing behind him. His feet turn into claws, his skin scaled and wet. Somehow I'm down the stairs now, walking toward him, those black eyes so hypnotic and commanding. The maple tree in the yard starts to glow, changing from green to amber, rustling in the breeze and sighing, "Keep going now." Just a few more steps, and I'll be in the garden with him. Will we tango, will we laugh, will we make it?

My feet are in the garden's soil. I am so close to him. He's just a few breaths in front of me.

A clicking noise snaps my attention upward. I see Jeremy in his bedroom window, watching me before he disappears.

I'm still standing in the garden, but he's gone now. The demon isn't here, maybe wasn't ever here. I am alone.

A scream sends me spinning. Jeremy is in the doorframe, his terrified mother beside him. He's holding Jack's gun, at Jack's head.

Blood rains, and my whale dies.

I run. I can't feel my feet moving. I'm in a field, with weeds tall and fuzzy, itching all the way through my jeans. I could run to the road, I could run back to my car, but I should run, run, run. I stumble a dozen times, maybe two dozen times, the ground so uneven and soupy. There is a terrible buzzing in the field, insects at war or at least as mad as they've ever been. So mad, just like Jack's mother was. I don't look behind me. There's a clearing in the woods, I see it while I'm running, and so I run that way, not knowing where it goes, not knowing if he's behind me, after me, going to kill me, too. He'd have a pretty open shot in this field.

I turn at a big rock covered in what looks like burn marks. There's a dusty trail in the woods, made of two narrow lines and grass growing in-between. It meanders through the trees and down, down, down, right to a river. It's strange to see such beauty adjacent to the crumbling trailer park. I bet Jack came down here a lot growing up. It almost feels like another place, another state or country. I can hear frogs, and a gentle whoosh as cattails wiggle and sway on the edge of the water. Lily pads are placed just so, calmly floating and wondering what all the fuss is about on land. This is a place where poets come to write, I think, and musicians learn to make new music.

Now I dare to look behind me. No one has followed me. I crumble on the bank and come undone, shocked and terrified and desperately sad. I will wake up tomorrow, and this won't have happened. I shake on the clumpy grass, convincing myself that this is so. Tomorrow I'll help Jack load his boxes and we'll wave goodbye, maybe one last hug in the driveway. Then everything will just be like it was before I met him, before he came to college and into my life. I'll have my quiet, my peace, in my still home, with my space back and daily routine and there won't be any of this to preoccupy my mind or heart. Jack will be down in Chicago, analyzing music scores and wondering where to grab dinner in the city. Maybe I'll visit him from time to time, come to a performance or two. Maybe we can just chat, like we used to, about worldly and science concerns instead of our own. Then I'll laugh and he'll smile and we'll look out over the Chicago skyline and think we're such lucky fools for getting the life we wanted. He'll confess to me that he's finally happy. My parents will still be dead, the ice skater will still be dead, but he'll be alive.

Now I can't process more than one second at a time. What am I supposed to do? I can't just go home. I can't just stand up and walk back through the woods, through the field, to my car . . . can I? Should I? Certainly someone heard the shots. Certainly someone called the police, called an ambulance.

My tears cover me like a cloth, falling onto my arms and legs. I never knew how bad things were for Jack. So often we only talked about me, because I'm selfish and self-absorbed. I can't believe he's gone, just like that, while I stood by, then simply ran off. Seems I'm always running off. And now I've lost him.

CHAPTER 17

I'm ambling along the river's edge. I sat by the bank for hours, I think, though I have no watch on my wrist today. Dusk is threatening to give in to night now. I spent my time sitting there, completely dumbfounded, as nature subtly changed around me. It's so peaceful by the water. Strange that I haven't spent more time just sitting in my backyard, watching the water behind my house shift and dazzle. Because that's wasting time, I always say. Actively do something, don't just sit. God, for one more night with Jack. We'd just sit and enjoy, nothing more, and that would be plenty.

The further south I walk, the thinner the trees look. Now I can make out porch lights from the distant trailer park, little white dots among the leaves. If I stop I can hear a light clanging, like a birdhouse rattling on a pole or someone rolling up their hose. Twigs snap under my feet. I don't feel afraid anymore, even though it's getting too dark to see the little path and I have no idea what's become of Jack's brother or his mother or any of that. I don't know if the police came. I don't know if Jeremy ran in the other direction, or used that gun again. I've thought about every possibility the last few hours. I thought about all of my options over and over too, and none of them feel right or safe except to just keep walking. And as I walk, I wonder how Jeremy managed to pick up Jack's gun.

Eventually the path broadens into a new lane, one that seems to be decidedly going somewhere. The river starts to zigzag away from me, rolling down another direction. I feel safe by the water, but if this lane is a road out I should take it. My walk becomes easy now, and I realize the lane is paved. The air turned heavy and damp some time ago, but currently it's tinged with the smell of gas and meat and charcoal. Voices carry faintly over the pavement, colliding with me in gentle bursts. I grow suspicious, thinking of this area as it'd look on a map. I think I've been down here before. It's very dark, but there's an outline of something familiar nearby. As I approach, I see the motionless swings and metal slide, still dented and still empty. Soon enough the campground sign hangs overhead, the one where Jack and I stopped for a picture. And I wonder, immediately and urgently, if Jack played down here as a kid. If he ran around at night, seeing all the families camping, wishing he were one of the kids cuddled up to his parents with a fishing pole by his feet.

"Unbelievable," I whisper. We were so close to his old trailer the first time we were down here together. He never said a word. Had we stopped at the trailer then, what would have happened? Would Jack have died before today? Already in the ground, a funeral program tucked away in my nightstand drawer?

The pavement thins to dirt, into one big dusty ring thrown around the RVs and pop-up tents. There's a family camping near the entrance. A little boy is bustling about in turtle pajamas, his silhouette coming and going through the light of the fire. His sister, presumably, is nearby in a reclined lawn chair, reading aloud from a big picture book with a flashlight in hand. Her mother sits close, leaning over and smoothing her hair.

"And then the geeses—"

"The geese," her mother corrects.

"And then the geese went to the pond. They started driving—"

"Diving."

"They started diving into the water."

I'm strongly enchanted by the scene, almost paralyzed, watching this young girl learning how to read, watching this young family on vacation, as I stand unseen in the darkness. I can hear her little breaths, all her little inflections. I can see her static-risen hair and a bit of dinner left on her face. Her toes are curling and uncurling as she concentrates, as she carefully tries to get everything just right. I'm watching a memory for this family, one the mother will think about as her children grow, and leave, and go off to do whatever good work or madness beckons stronger.

Just as my mind starts a deeper dangerous wander, the little girl says, "Hey, there's a lady out there!"

I am startled, and still. I can't run off, but I can't just stand here, like a weird voyeur watching young children. Feeling sick all over again, I walk into the light of their fire, like the guilty turning themselves in.

"Nice night for camping," I say awkwardly, rather dumbly. Thankfully, the family smiles at me. The children seem especially interested in me, actually excited to see me, like I'm some aunt.

"Are you camping here, too?" the boy wants to know.

What to say? "Not today," I tell him, trying to look very normal and harmless. "I'm just taking a walk."

The little girl nods, like she's got it all figured out. "You must just be visiting," she says with certainty. "Sometimes our Grandma comes to visit us when we're camping. Do you want a hamburger?"

All of those proverbs about innocent children seem pretty accurate, I surmise, standing in this difficult night west of Ann Arbor. And of course, I can't help but wonder if I acted like this at her age. Presumably I did. My eyes drift to the parents, looking so pleased with their child's hospitality, looking so alive and full of genuine contentment. We used to camp near a picturesque stream in Wisconsin, one that had horses nearby that I got to ride in the mornings. I was so excited to ride those horses, excited over them for days beforehand. I remember now.

The mother says to me, "You know, you can certainly have a hamburger. We're going to toss them anyway. Should I wrap one in a napkin for your walk?"

I haven't eaten yet, during this endless second half of the day. "If you're just going to throw them out, I suppose I should," I tell her, still trying to seem normal and human and just anything but what I'm feeling right now. The father quickly flips open the family's blue cooler on wheels and fishes out a beer for me. "Will this do to drink?"

I guess I don't look like a troublemaker or I wouldn't get a Bud. I'm really quite harmless from the outside. "That'd be great," I tell him.

The father peers around me and smiles. "Does your friend want dinner, too?"

I turn as fast as a pinwheel, as blank and confused as a newborn. Jeremy is only a few steps behind me, where the fire's light just ends, his body just an undefined gray smudge. I'm certain that he's staring at me. I've never felt closer to death.

"I'm good," he tells the father. "Just ate, actually."

I receive my hamburger and the family waves and gets back to the business of the evening, which is simply playing and reading and enjoying each other's company. I have to do something. I have to get Jeremy away from here. These children, they can't watch this. A fearful moan escapes my throat and I approach Jeremy. He puts a heavy, foreign arm around my shoulder and leads me further into the campground. He feels nothing like his brother. His skin is different, and his soul, so very different.

"You're shaking," he says.

"Are you going to kill me?" I whisper.

"I haven't decided yet," Jeremy says. "I don't know you as well as I want to, Mae."

So I guess things could go either way.

"Eat your burger. Drink your beer," he instructs. "Sure is a nice night to grill out."

I do both as his arm continues to push down on my shoulders. "Romantic, ain't it?" he laughs, steering me out of the campground and up the long driveway entrance. I hope for a passing car that pulls into the campground after a dinner in town. Then I pray for a passing car, please please please, someone please send me a car, Jesus now is the time. But it's a still and warm evening, a perfectly lovely night, one that campers probably wouldn't want to waste inside a restaurant. I'm sure all the campers are doing just what that family was doing: enjoying the site they paid for.

There's one last lamplight at the top of the driveway, then dark nothingness. I steal a glance behind me and can just make out a silvery glimpse of the river. Oh, had I just followed the river, I start to realize. But, maybe I'd already be dead if I'd gone that route. These what-if scenarios around death have been plaguing me a long time, since that night on the bridge as a teenager. Actually, I started thinking about my own death one night in sixth grade, at a local roller rink. That's when I realized I would die one day, while just lazily making circles around and around with other ponytailed girls as our parents watched on, and I was so sick over the matter I threw up on the car ride home.

"Jack and I rode bikes around here when we were kids," he tells me.

That old drained swimming pool and boarded-up supply store is just a short walk away, I remember. We passed it after we took our picture in the campground. I'm sure Jeremy is unaware that I've been here before. It's very dark now, but it's clear no one uses the road we're on very much, which is so laden with potholes and fallen branches that we've been taking turns stumbling for the past few minutes.

"How did you get Jack's gun?" I ask, staying very direct with Jeremy. I don't want to hear about Jack's childhood right now. It's pretty clear Jeremy isn't the regretful kind.

"Ah, well, that's one of the guns I'm carrying. I've got two in case you want to try to defend yourself. That seems fair. As for Jack's gun, turns out family gets first dibs on jail property," he says with an untrusting smile.

"You're not real," I tell him, but neither of us believes it.

When I was a new teacher, still finishing up grad school, the university used to teach us how to spot troubled individuals and refer them to the "appropriate agency" before they caused any damage, whether to themselves or fellow students. Well, I've spotted one. Too bad training stopped at the referring stage.

I think when you're in a hostage situation, which might be what I'm in right now, you're supposed to keep the bad guy talking, supposed to make him see that you're not worth killing and that his life is worth saving, too. I think Jack would have a better chance at this than I would. "I loved riding bikes with you," he could say. "Remember how we had to steer with one hand, because we had popsicles in the other—grape for you, orange for me?" Jeremy would listen, growing interested at the first person to acknowledge his preferences in life. "Remember how we climbed that sandy 'mountain' near the trailer park, and found that cool blue rock? Remember how we thought that if we just turned it over, the sky would open and grant us one wish each? And when it didn't happen, we thought it was because we had to wash the rock first? We ran all the way back home and used the hose, but forgot to turn it off and it flooded all the way out to the main road before we were home again."

At this point, Jeremy might add, "That's because we had to watch ourselves all day and night because Mom worked three jobs, or she would have turned the hose off." And I suppose this realization could go either way—Jeremy could get mad all over again, or maybe start to feel grateful that he had his brother for a companion growing up. Everyone knows siblings can go either way: that you can really luck out or you can have a lifelong personal enemy.

All of this could happen, if Jack were here. He's not, but one of us still is.

I punch Jeremy in the side of the face so hard that he collapses to the ground with a tremendous scream and thump. My hand might be broken, because I'm numb up to my elbow. This is the first time I've hit anyone. I'm glad it worked. I want to keep hitting him, push my strappy sandal into his throat and listen to him choke, make him hurt over Jack, maybe even kill him for Jack. But I know I have to run again, and so I do.

I hear only myself as I travel the dusty road lined with impressive black evergreens: my labored breathing, dirt kicking up behind me, little smacks and crunches underfoot, continual little stumbles. It's so dark now, the moon completely gone behind the atmosphere, that I could run right into anything, and I nearly do slam into the chain link fence around the old swimming pool. My hand throbs now that I've stopped running. I cough and spit up from stress. The warm saliva on my chin tastes like blood and meat.

I grope along the metal. There's loose concrete everywhere here, some like little boulders, and I just can't imagine how one could abandon a whole complex: a pool, a store, a huge firewood pile. Why not sell it? Where do the campers go now? Do they really have to drive all the way back to Ann Arbor?

Am I going to get to drive back to Ann Arbor?

Surely Jeremy is close. I suspect he's quite close, and is being very quiet out here, which is what I should do now. He could be just a few steps behind me, carefully stepping over the broken concrete, too. I listen. Nothing but the quiet rustle of nature right now.

I could try to hide in the boarded-up store, but the very idea has me shaking from claustrophobia, from waiting for pain, hunger, thirst, death. I don't want to be in this horror story. As I round the corner to the long end of the pool, walking with light feet and a spinning brain, I start to think very critically about the possibility that Jeremy is a demon. His body, just a frumpy teenager, with pus-zits and gel-hair, able to transform into scales with a tail. His eyes, not human. His agenda, working right for the devil. Is this possible? Some people believe in ghosts. Some people believe in aliens. Is the devil with me tonight? I may never know.

As I pat along the rotting wood of the old camping store with the hand that doesn't hurt, feeling little knotholes and picking up rouge splinters, I contemplate my unstable mind. I'm starting to wonder if I'm human myself, or at best, if this is all some kind of hallucination. Sandy dirt outside the door makes me sink with each step, and I cry as I move on, silent and pained. I take little sneaks over my shoulder, but there's nothing to see. It's like hiking the desert at night, weary of snakes and animal burrows underfoot and even a little cactus attaching to your ankle. I wonder if Jack took any vacations at all growing up, or if this little store and pool was the only thing he looked forward to visiting.

There are ripped garbage bags over the windows, some flapping like tattered flags. I grab one just long enough to peek inside through a little corner hole. But there's still nothing to see. I creep around the corner and find the front of the store properly boarded up, but with a perfectly nice ice machine sitting out front, its cord plugged in and the metal box gently buzzing. There's a dim light here, coming from a nearby streetlight next to the store's driveway. The front door of the place seems to have a new handle, too. I keep walking and see about a dozen buckets of paint lined up and an open toolbox. So it seems another generation of campers and trailer park dwellers will get to come down here during the muggy Michigan summers. I slip a utility knife into my pocket from the toolbox, feeling just a little guilty for stealing this time.

Every shaking instinct tells me not to walk down the lit driveway, but my brain tells me it's a way out of the woods, and I've got to get out of this endless woods. A car is parked at the end of the driveway, and as I approach, legs wobbling and breath short, I'm convinced the headlights will flick on and Jeremy will run me over. Or maybe the car will grow silvery wings and fly away. I've read that sometimes the devil appears as an angel, a trusting soul to lure the naive into his controlling fists. I see the car is the same kind—a Mercury Grand Marquis—that I drove off the bridge that summer. It's surprising to see one again. This one is in pretty good shape for its age.

"I didn't get to know your heart well, but I do know a lot about your life," he says, crazily close to my body.

My legs buckle. I can't see Jeremy; I can only hear him, so close.

"Don't faint, I can't catch you. I'm pretty fucking banged up here."

When my parents died, I knew the exact moment they took their last breaths. I couldn't see them, under the water, under that bridge, but I knew when they left. I felt my mother and my father in my veins; saw their memories, before I was born, in my mind. Some people inherit money when their parents die, and I'm one of them. But I also inherited their knowledge, and their unfinished plans. I felt their souls fuse into mine as they passed, and now these souls are in danger again.

"I've been in your room," he starts again. "While you were fucking my brother, my mother and I were suffering in that shit hole, cursing you and him and hoping the very worst for you both."

"I never—" I whisper, but stop when I feel his arm brush against me.

And as quick as anything, I'm not afraid anymore. Just calm, and ready. "So this is the way we're going to leave," I say. "I suppose you're going to shoot me first, then kill yourself."

"Do you miss him?" he asks. "Do you already miss Jack?"

"Absolutely."

"Do you want his gun, and I'll take my own? Do you want a chance to take my life first? But either way, I'll be seeing you in Hell, Mae. Jack's already waiting for us. Why do you think he had a gun, Mae? Was it to kill you?"

I hear him slide both guns from his pockets, the metal of the barrels reuniting in his hands. Jack belongs here, not him. My parents belong here, not me. I look up, straining to see a star, or the moon, or anything in this moment of absolute aloneness. Jeremy drops in the bullets, clicks everything neatly into place, and exhales.

The car's headlights snap on. Captain Douglas springs from the Marquis, trying to make it over in time. I turn to Jeremy, anxious to finally look at Satan in all his lively madness. Jeremy looks at me, seems nearly remorseful, oddly pained. He lifts both guns to his head and pulls those easy little levers. Blood rains again, and his soul sinks down, gone for good now.

CHAPTER 18

I've never needed much in the way of special occasion wear. I never got married, so I never needed the fancy white dress, and I've only attended one wedding in my thirty-six years. I never had kids, and thus never needed fancy clothes for their baptisms or birthdays or recitals. Sometimes I dress up for college graduations, but not really dress up with nice jewelry, because students aren't relation, and they aren't supposed to be permanent in my life. But today, I'm standing in my closet, my hand flipping through old dresses to see if I have anything special enough for Jack and Jeremy's funeral.

I choose a basic blue dress, knowing my attire doesn't matter. I fumble as I take it off the hanger because of my wrapped hand. I'm thinking only of his mother now. I could be thinking about how I'll ever return to normalcy at the university and especially my now quiet home, or about what I'm going to do with all of Jack's boxes that I don't think his mother wants, but today, a mother is attending a double funeral for her sons, one of whom shot the other before shooting himself. And even though she was a bad mother, that's still about the heaviest thing I can imagine happening to another human. And so, I mourn; less for me, and more for her, even though I miss Jack with a pain so severe I know I'll never recover.

The light material of my dress gets caught on my monitoring anklet. As I carefully pull out the hem, I realize that I've only ever been to one funeral, too, and it was also a double funeral. Pam and I have more in common than I'd like to think about today.

I creak down my stairs and walk into Jack's old room. This task bothered me all night, as much as thinking about attending his funeral. I bend down to lift the oil painting I bought in Chicago, the one of the nice little cottage house from the estate sale. I affix it to a nail above Jack's old bed. It seems like the kind of house he'd have liked to call his own. It's not a picture of my parents on the wall. It's not a picture of Jack on the wall. But it's important to me that it's up on this wall. With the edge of my fingernail, I scratch little dings into the paint onto the house's shutters. "There," I say aloud. "There's something for you to fix, Jack."

I hold my phone as I leave the room. "Hi, Mae Harrington, calling to remind my parole officer that I have a funeral to attend today."

Papers rustle in the background. "Yes, that's approved. You can leave your house. Just be back in three hours."

"Thank you."

Oscar pads in as I'm pouring a quick cup of tea, his tail low, his eyes droopy. He's been spending a lot of time sitting out on the pier lately, but not watching for fish or bugs, just watching the air, the sky. I wonder if he knows that Jack is gone. I scratch his chin. His eyes close.

"I'll be back soon," I tell him, sliding my keys into my purse. "I have to be."

My neighborhood is still today, with just a few people shuffling around outside to scoop up papers or waste time pruning shrubs before church. Mr. Wright, the last neighbor on my street, warmly waves to me as I turn away from home. I wave back, surprised to receive positive attention. I single-handedly turned a comfortable, leafy neighborhood of a hundred houses into a non-stop neighborhood watch, with police and constant suspicions and the occasional demon peddling on his bike. I'm embarrassed. I want to give these last days and weeks back to my neighbors who were otherwise looking forward to their summers by the water, give them glasses of sweating lemonade, loud laughter on the deck over corn on the cob, and evening baseball games over the radio. Mr. Wright gives me hope that I can give this all back soon.

I'm leaving out the other side of town, the side that doesn't lead to Jack's old trailer park and the campground. Recently Ann Arbor was classified as a suburb of Detroit, which I'm choosing not to believe. Because moments after leaving town, I'm again among flat fields stuffed with purple wildflowers, and thick trees that look like Heaven's fence posts stuck into the soil. I never go into Detroit if I can help it. But here, I'd like to stay right here all day.

Soon I'm exiting onto a gravel road and checking the paper clipping to make sure I'm headed in the right direction. I'm looking for Holy Redeemer, as specified in Jack's obituary, but there isn't much out here except little houses on huge lots with leaning mailboxes. I drive on, wondering why the funeral wasn't held closer to home.

And then, I've arrived, pulling into the country church's parking lot. I'm relieved to see dozens, maybe close to a hundred cars here, and start wondering how big Jack's family really is, and what Pam's community is like. Sadly, I know there aren't any of Jack's friends here, unless a few old flames decided to show up for a good closure cry. In the years he lived at my house, the phone rarely rang for him.

The tears fall.

I walk up the cement stairs and into the sanctuary. The scene is arresting: quiet, somber organ music playing, people hugging, light from the stained glass windows pooling right on top of two matching caskets. I recognize the backs of Sam and Julie a few pews in, and I think to myself: haven't I called them since we ate breakfast together? What kind of a friend am I?

I look around, try to take it all in, try to process this end, and notice the Stations of the Cross on the walls. And the Catholic iconography, everywhere, relentless while surrounding those gathered between. When my eyes meet Mary's, I panic.

Jack wouldn't want a Catholic funeral. Do I do something? Do I say something? Surely his mother wouldn't think a Catholic funeral, of all rituals, would be appropriate for her atheist son. And it's allowed for her murdering son?

But apparently Pam didn't know Jack the way that I knew Jack. And this is a funeral, not a planned party. I realize that I'm a guest here, probably an uninvited guest, and take a seat in the back for the service. I scan the funeral's program, printed on ivory paper with a phrase stating, "We adore our deceased as we adore Christ." I nearly work myself up again when I see that Jack will be buried behind the church, in the Holy Redeemer Cemetery, but calm myself down as the priest takes his place up front. I guess someone in his family went to services here, I guess his extended family was Catholic, and as I ponder this, I recall Jack saying that sometimes his mother would leave him and his brother home alone on Sunday mornings. "We'd try to just sleep, but really we'd lie awake and wonder why we couldn't go along." Oh, the conversations Jack and I still had coming.

A mother wails. I see Pam's hair first, tied in a graying knot between the shoulders of two women leaning into her. Her hair looks wet, and her black and plum dress, freshly pressed. She turns toward the priest, and I see her splotchy face in profile. Now I'm back at my own parents' funeral, back when things were just a "tragic accident in our community," and I was just a kid, unable to think of anything except having to return to my foster family after the burial, but only until college started in a few weeks. Somehow, it felt like I'd see my mom and dad again, maybe not for a while, but I'd see them again. There is a pain, sometimes an acute pain in my stomach, that visits me often.

I'm so relieved the caskets are closed.

The priest lifts his hands as the church bows their heads. "Friends, family," he begins. "We've had a tragic event in our community. And now, in this Mass, we must pray for safe passages, we must pray for their souls and the forgiving heart of our Lord."

Pam is roused in the front, visibly swaying in her seat and shaking her head. Everyone cries together, in a sound like a broken orchestra. There are prayers, many of them, some spoken and hundreds silent. There are songs, and readings from the Gospels, and a few short remarks about grief from the priest, who is too affected to do much other than watch the caskets, his eyes so heavy.

As it all washes over me, I notice Captain Douglas sitting a few pews ahead, his shoulders stiff, his head down. He turns to look out a sunny side window and his skin illuminates in the rays. His face tells a story I know so well, one of a person bearing the kind of guilt that falls on top of you and slowly strangles, the guilt of not having done enough.

And then the brokenhearted rise and look on as the pallbearers, people I've never seen before, lift away two boys and take them out the double doors and into the morning sunshine, a line of people starting to file out behind them. As I think and cry, now so somber and unstable that I'm sure I just heard Jack's clarinet in the choir loft above me, I think maybe it's good that these two have a little religion in their afterlives, nestled among the cement crosses in Christ's shadow.

When I've broken out of my spell enough to finally get up and head to the cemetery, I see Pam is still in the church, still between the women taking care of her. I want to go to her so desperately; she deserves my humbleness, and my condolences now. Shaking the whole way, I walk along the middle aisle to see her, my gaze averting the tempting altar that's gotten me into trouble so many times before.

"I'm not going home again, I can't go home again," she tells the women. "That will never be my home again."

I can't get close to her. My feet are stitched into the carpet, and I feel the eyes of a thousand on me, telling me now is not the time. As I stand there, the priest comes back into the church. "Pam," he says softly, "we're about to begin the burial rites. Do you want to come outside?"

She rises from the pew. I follow steps behind the others, casting one last look around the church before I leave completely. It feels hard to leave somehow, even though I know Jack isn't here, and that I shouldn't stand around such temptation. But I'm confident I won't steal from churches again. This brick building can't save me. Now I know.

As the doors click close and the church falls silent, the Apostles on the wall, stone here instead of the usual plastic in other small churches, close their watchful eyes.

I'm the last one to get to their graves, a purposeful straggler trying to not interfere too much in this gathering. At times during the service I tried to convince myself that I deserve to be here as much as anyone—that Jack was my friend—but he was also my tenant, and my student, and there is family here. They may wonder who I am. And if they find out, I don't think things will go so well. Couldn't I have done more to save him? Why did I leave those trailer porch steps, why did I leave him that night when he needed me most? This is a guilt I will carry forever, until I am in the ground, until the moon falls into the ocean.

Everyone is huddled close, but the group respectfully opens when Pam approaches to let her get to the front, the way people at a wedding stand when the bride appears. I stop at the edge of the group, my hands folded, now just waiting for this to be done.

The priest continues with his rites, his prayers, his visible uncomfortableness and sorrow over all this. As I stand here, at once wanting to throw myself on the coffin but also to drive off and away, away, away, I think of Young Jack versus Old Jack: Jack as a college freshman and Jack as an emerging adult. I manage to think of Jack's transition from the always-flippant college guy to our Jack, my Jack, with great talent and promise, for most of the burial in the cemetery. He was on the upswing, and I can picture him ten years from now, twenty years from now, better with age, like we always talked about for me. But soon enough, as the leafy ground rustles and the earth seems to shift from the souls of these brothers leaving separate ways, I think about our quiet times, our intimate times. He was my student, as I've said so many times now. But he was my friend, I let myself admit, and my admirer, and to him, he was also my protector. He really cared about me. I could have cared a little more. I was sick, and he wanted to make me better. And today, we were in church together.

I pray a long and pleading prayer for Jack. I do hope that his afterlife, in whatever sort of new neighborhood he ends up in, is particularly kind, with a nice wooden clarinet to play, one with a smooth, deep tone. He didn't believe, but I do.

The group breaks up now, distraught and still weeping couples heading back to their cars. Pam is kneeling next to the loose piles of dirt, as she must do in her flower garden in front of her trailer. She shouldn't be here any longer. She shouldn't stare at their new graves, wishing her boys would just float up and be with her again.

And then I hear her, still so frantic. "I can't go back home. I can never go back there. Where am I supposed to go? I have no where to go." The women are rubbing her back, but not providing any answers.

Out here, it seems easy to walk to her. "Pam?" I say quietly.

She looks up, and I brace myself, not sure what kind of reaction I'll receive. Her head tips to the side and her eyes spark with recognition.

"Oh, you're here," her voice cracks out. "I didn't know you were here."

Our eyes fall to the graves in unison. She surprises me with, "Thank you for coming. Jack loved you."

I don't know how to respond. So I say nothing.

"Can you believe all this?" she says, not sounding at all like the fierce and tortured woman I met last week. "My babies," she trails off. In a moment, she is sobbing again. "I can't go back. I have no home."

Death changes everything.

I don't know where this answer comes from. But as I'm crouching next to Jack's mother, feeling all the weight of her sorrow, watching the priest walk away, I say, "Would you like to stay at my place for a while? Sort things through?"

My question startles her. Then, an introspective look crosses her face. "You know, I never got to see where Jack lived in college, even though he was so close. Just a few miles away. I really wanted to."

I'm the reason she didn't get to. I think about everything I could show her: a campus tour, the river behind my house that Jack liked so much, the pier he fixed for me, maybe even play her some of his music, give her his clarinet. Maybe this will give her the closure she needs for being an absent mother. Maybe this will give me the closure I need for not appreciating Jack when I had him.

"You're welcome today or another day."

"I'll come right now," she says, pulling herself to a stand.

And just like that, a part of Jack returns to me.

ACKNOWLEDGEMENTS

My gratitude to my patient husband, Adam, for sharing head space with these characters, and to Aunt Nancy for spending her life building up the lives of her family. Thanks to Autumn Harting for her warm assistance and revision support, and to Nikki, Elizabeth, Kathleen, and Cheryl for walking beside me during this process. Thanks also to Carl Stratman for copyediting, and Kristin Mitchell for her editorial coordination and enthusiasm.

Finally, thank you to my little love letters Josie and Chelsea for letting their mother "type" so much.